DICK'S FAIRY

"What is it?" asked Dick,

DICK'S FAIRY

A TALE OF VICTORIAN MANCHESTER

by

SILAS K. HOCKING

GALLERY PRESS
LIVERPOOL

© Original Edition : Frederick Warne & Co.

© This Edition :   The Gallery Press
                   Seel House
                   Seel Street
                   Liverpool L1 4AY

ISBN 0 900389 16 8

SEEL HOUSE PRESS LTD.
LIVERPOOL L1 4AY

CONTENTS

		Page
I	THE LITTLE RUNAWAY	9
II	LUTHER'S QUEST	16
III	DICK'S GLUEPOT	23
IV	LOST, STOLEN OR STRAYED	29
V	LUTHER AS A PRIVATE DETECTIVE	35
VI	GATHERING CLOUDS	43
VII	"MISSING"	49
VIII	A DISCOVERY	56
IX	SUSPENSE	64
X	A FRESH CLUE	72
XI	AN ACCIDENT	81
XII	EXPLANATIONS	91
XIII	AT LAST	100
XIV	WELCOME HOME	109
XV	LIGHT IN DARKNESS	117
XVI	CHANGES	127
XVII	AND LAST	135

I

THE LITTLE RUNAWAY

THEIR MEETING WAS A strange one. They were both running at full speed, and in opposite directions. *He* tattered, hungry, and cold; *she* gaudily dressed, hot, and excited. He was running with a careless swing and a heart that was light in spite of his poverty and rags; she was bounding on like a haunted hare, with every sense keenly awake and eyes ready to start out of their sockets. He was running towards his home; she away from hers. He was anxious to get warm; she to get out of sight.

The streets were dark and the corner sharp, and so they met full tilt. Before either had time to get out of the way of the other, the inevitable collision occurred. A simultaneous "Oh!" burst from their lips, and the younger and weaker staggered back a few steps and fell to the ground.

He was by her side in a moment, and had caught her up in his arms.

"I'm so sorry, my little gal," he said; "are ye hurt?"

"No, not very much," she said, "but let me go, please, I's in a hurry."

"In a hurry, are you?" and he placed her gently on the ground, but kept her hands still in his. But she did not seem very eager to get away.

"Perhaps you're goin' home?" he asked.

"Oh, no, I'm not," she said quickly. "I'm—I'm—but who are you?"

He laughed a little at that, and let go her hands. "I'm Dick Dugdale," he said, "and live at Fourteen Tinker's Row."

"Don't know where that is," she said; "but hush! there's footsteps, they're after me," and she drew back into the shadow of the tall building.

"It's only a Bobby," he said; "but what are ye so frightened at?"

"I don't like the pleece," she said. "Last time as I runned away one on 'em took me back again."

Dick gave a low whistle at this. "So you've runned away, 'ave yer?" he said after a pause.

"Ay," she said in a whisper, "but *you'll* not tell on me, will yer? You're not a Bobby."

"But 'taint right to run away from yer home," he said, "and ye're sich a little dot. An' what'll yer mother think when she finds out?"

"But she ain't my mother," was the answer, "she's told me lots of times I ain't got no mother nor father, they's both dead an' in the ground."

"Poor little gal," said Dick in a tone of sympathy, "them's 'ard lines." She began to cry at this, and Dick caught her up in his arms again. "Don't fret, little gal," he said, "I'll not tell on yer. But what are 'e agoin' to do, wi' no home to go to?"

"Oh, I don't know," she answered, "anywheres is better'n goin' back again. She 'most killed me last time as I run away, an' I'd rather let a 'bus run over me than I'd go back."

"It's a queer pickle, anyhow," said Dick. "I'd take yer to our house on'y it 'ud be no use."

"Why?" she asked, simply.

"Cause mother's ill and couldn't look after 'e; besides,

we're so mighty poor. But we must be movin, out o' this, for I'm 'most froze."

"Ye're terrible ragged," she said, with engaging frankness; "my clothes is ever so much nicer."

"Gals' clothes is cheap, I specks," he answered; "an' then mother ain't able to do no mendin' scarce. But what's the hodds 'bout a few ribbons? besides, wentilation is good, so folks say; and when I gets to be a gentleman I'll smarten up a mite."

"Are ye goin' to be a gentleman some day?"

"Mos' likely—no knowin'—nothin' sartin—nothin' like hopin', anyhow."

This conversation was carried on while running side by side through a narrow and badly-lighted street. At length she drew back suddenly with a little cry of fear. They had reached the end of the narrow street, and were about to cross a broad and well-lighted thoroughfare.

"What is it?" asked Dick, in some alarm, when his companion drew back so suddenly.

"Mrs. Limber," she gasped. "She's after me. Oh, what shall I do if she sees me?"

"Don't you never fear," said Dick, stoutly. "Is that her wi' the red shawl?"

"Ay, that's her."

"Oh, well, she ain't seen us," was the reassuring answer; "an' she'll soon be out of sight. You just stand behind me till I give the word, then bolt across like greased lightnin'."

In a few minutes the glaring thoroughfare was safely crossed, and they were in comparative darkness once more. For some distance they hurried on in silence. Then she looked up in his face with the question, "Where are ye a-takin' me to?"

"Dunno yet. I'll call on Luther first, an' ax him what

he thinks."

"Who's Luther?"

"Oh, he's an old cove 'as lives in next street to ourn."

"Is he nice?"

"No, not very. He's a curious owd blade, but he's mighty knowin', an' he's good at bottom, though you wouldn't think so to hear 'im talk."

"What does he do?"

"Oh, he mends shoes mostly, when he ain't makin' new ones, which ain't very often."

"He's got a queer name, anyhow."

"Oh, Luther's only part of his name; his proper name's Luther Cob. That's 'cause he's a cobbler, don't 'e see?"

"Not very well, an' I don't want to see him."

"You needn't fear," was the reply, "he ain't haaf a bad sort when you git to know 'im. He's queer, awful queer, but you mustn't take no notice. You jist trust yourself to me, an' I'll take care of ye, never fear."

"You don't think he'll take me to Mrs. Limber, do ye?"

"Sartin he won't, so keep your heart up, little gal, for 'ere we are," and Dick raised the latch of Luther's door without ceremony, and marched boldly in, closely followed by the little girl.

There was no one in the outer room, which answered the double purpose of workshop and showroom. On the little counter an oil lamp was burning dimly, revealing a number of shoe-lasts, tips, and scraps of leather, while before the window, on a slanting shelf, was a curious assortment of second-hand boots and shoes exposed for sale. These, during the day, were carried outside the window, to be examined and bargained for by those who wanted something cheap in shoe-leather, and were not particular about the fit.

"Luther's finished work for the day, I 'spect," Dick whispered to his companion, "so you'd better stay 'ere a bit, and I'll go inter the back room an' 'ave a crack wi' him about what's to be done."

It was not without considerable misgiving, however, that Dick obtruded himself upon Luther's presence. He knew that the old man was no lover of children, and that he hated to be disturbed, especially in the evenings, when his day's work was done. For nearly forty years Luther had lived alone. It is said that in his young days he had seriously contemplated marriage, and would in all probability have taken a wife had not the young woman of his choice got married to another man. Since then Luther had lived almost a hermit's life. Two or three times a week an old woman came in to tidy up his home, but Luther always seemed ill at ease when she was about, and was always glad to be alone again. Dick had known Luther ever since he could remember, and was about the only lad in the neighbourhood that could be considered to be on friendly terms with the old man. Indeed, most of the lads were Luther's avowed enemies, and rarely lost an opportunity of showing their dislike.

"I wonder what the owd bloke will say?" was Dick's reflection, as he slowly pushed open the door that separated the shop from the living-room. He felt somehow as if he had come on a fool's errand. What business had he to take up with a runaway child, and encourage her in trying to hide from her friends? How did he know that she had told him the truth? Was not her running away the stupid freak of a wayward child, that ought not to be encouraged for a moment? And was it not more than likely that Mrs. Limber was her own mother, and was now perhaps, almost distracted at her absence? These thoughts rushed through Dick's mind with lightning speed, and almost staggered him for a moment. It was only for a moment, however. There was something about this little waif that touched his heart strangely. There was such a look of terror in her eyes when she stumbled across him, such a ring of sincerity in the tones of her voice when she spoke, such evident dread of going back again, that Dick couldn't help but believe that her story was true. "She's been badly used, 'as the little gal," was his reflection, "an' I'll help her all I can," and he marched boldly into Luther's presence. The room was full of the warm glow of the firelight, for Luther believed in making himself comfortable when his day's work was over, and was now seated in a large easy chair, with a clay pipe between his fingers, from which he pulled deep whiffs at rather long intervals.

"Well, lad, what's thy business?" he said, looking up as Dick entered.

"I wanted a word wi' you," said Dick, somewhat uneasily.

"A word wi' me! What about?"

"About a little gal as is waiting here in the shop."

"A little girl? Whose girl? What does she want?" And Luther glared at Dick in a way that was anything but reassuring.

"She ain't got no parents," stammered Dick, "and the people who keeps her abuses her, and she's runned away, an' she ain't no place to go to, and I meets her all alone in the street—"

"And you brought her here for me to keep?" snarled Luther. "Take her away this minute," And Luther got up from his chair and clenched his fist in a threatening attitude. "Do you think I'll harbour runaway children? Take her back to her home, and if she gets a hiding, sarves her right."

"But—but—" began Dick.

"No, not a 'but,' " snarled Luther. "Be gone this minute, or—"

But Dick did not wait to hear the end of the sentence; with a quick gesture he left the room and slammed the door behind him.

II

LUTHER'S QUEST

BEFORE DICK HAD TIME to open the shop door and get—with his little companion—into the street, Luther had thrown open the middle door, and was calling him back.

"What's the use o' coming back?" retorted Dick, who had his full share of spirit, and was highly indignant at the summary way in which he had been dismissed.

"Never mind what's the use," answered Luther; "you just do what I tell yer."

"There ain't no time to be wasted," Dick answered. "It's gettin' late, an' the little gal ain't no place to go to yet."

"Then come here, and bring the gal with you," snarled Luther; "an' don't waste no more time in chaffering."

"What shall we do?" said Dick, in a whisper, turning to his companion. "Shall we go back?"

"What! to Mrs. Limber?" she asked, in affright. "No, never. I'll go anywhere sooner than I'll go back again."

"I didn't mean that," he answered quickly. "I mean, shall we go into the room, as he wants?"

"I dunno," she said; "but I'll go anywhere wi' you."

"Come along, then," he answered. "He'll not eat us, an' the owd dog's bark is wus nor his bite any day." Saying which, he marched in after Luther, leading his companion by the hand.

"You can sit down here," said the old man, in kindlier

16

tones than he had before used, at the same time drawing up a large sofa in front of the fire. He then fetched the lamp from the shop, and placed it on the table. This done, he seated himself once more in his easy chair, and looked at the little girl for several seconds without speaking.

"Blamed if you're not a pretty little gal, anyhow," he said at length. "What's yer name?"

But a burst of tears was the only answer he got.

"Come, come, little gal, don't cry," he said in tones of distress. "I ain't used to seein' folks cry, and it boggles me somewhat. There, there, dry yer eyes. I'll not do 'e any harm if I knows it, so don't be skeared."

"I'm not skeared very much," she answered very dubiously, getting closer to Dick, whom she evidently regarded as her friend and champion.

"Well, well, I'm a bit of an old bear, I daresay," said Luther, "and I ain't no special love for children I admit, and I don't want to get inter trouble harbouring runaway brats; but 't ain't fair maybe to judge ye unheard, so dry yer eyes, little woman, an' tell us yer name."

"Fairy, sir," came the answer in timid tones.

"Fairy, eh? Fairy what?"

"Not anything else, sir."

"Nothing but Fairy? Well, that's queer. Where d'ye live?"

"Dunno, sir."

"Don't know? Come, come, ye must know." said Luther somewhat sternly.

"We shifts about so from place to place," said Fairy. "Sometimes I sleeps in the van, and sometimes in the tent. We're after the fairs mostly."

"Do ye belong to a show, then, or what?" asked Luther.

"Ay," said Fairy, brightening. "I'm the fairy. I dances

on the stage, and on the tight-rope, and acts Red Riding Hood, an' lots of things." Then her eyes filled with tears again. "But Mrs. Limber beats me awful when I don't do right; an' cause I tumbled off the rope to-night she kicked me, an' said I should get it worse before I slept, and so I slipped out under the canvas when nobody was lookin' and runned away."

"And so Mrs. Limber's yer mother, is she?" questioned Luther.

"Oh, no, she ain't," said Fairy, quickly. "She keeps a-tellin' me I'm a orphan brat. She says my mother's in the ground, and my father too."

"Oh, nonsense!" said Luther. "She's yer mother right enough, and you'll have to go back to her."

"Oh, no, I won't," said Fairy, her eyes dilating with fright, "She ain't my mother. If I calls her mother she tells me to shut up, an' says I'm a orphan brat that she's the keeping of. Oh, no, no! I'll never go back."

"But ain't there any Mr. Limber?" asked Luther.

"Ay, but he's mostly sick, an' is getting old, an' she serves him awful bad too sometimes. I like Mr. Limber very well. He talks nice to me when she ain't about, an' reads out o' the good book about God, an' all that."

"Bah!" said Luther; "but let that pass." And he got up and walked to the street door and opened it, and stood for some time looking out into the wintry night.

"Queer owd bloke, ain't he?" whispered Dick.

"Ay," she answered, placing her little hand in his. "P'r'aps he don't mean bad, though."

"No; he's right at bottom," Dick answered, "but he's curious ways wi' him. I wonder what he's a-thinkin' on standin' there i' t' cold?"

Luther came back after a bit, and carefully shut the

middle door. Dick and Fairy watched him narrowly for several seconds, wondering what was to be the next move.

"Look here," he said at length, "the night ain't fit to turn a dog out o' doors, and it's snowin' like—like—well, like—I'm blamed if I can find a word—well, it's snowin' like—like anything, there now. And if I ain't a saint I ain't a brute. So, little gal, you can stay here wi' me for the night, and sleep on the sofa, and ye'll be as warm as a kitten, I warrant, and nobody shall harm ye, there, now; an' to-morrow I'll inquire into the matter, blamed if I don't. Now, Dick, get thee home to thy mother, or she'll be thinkin' thou 'rt lost."

"Is Dick goin' away?" asked Fairy in alarm.

"Ay," said Luther. "He's got a mother to look after; but don't ye fear, nobody'll harm thee, little gal."

"But he'll come to see me again?" asked Fairy.

"Never fear," said Dick. "I'll be here to-morrow mornin' as soon's anybody's stirring. So keep yer heart up Fairy, an' Mrs. Limber 'll never catch ye again if I can 'elp it." And the next moment he was gone.

It was but a short distance to his own poor home. Before the merest glimmer of a fire, and by the light of a tallow candle, sat a thin pale woman, stitching away for dear life. This was Dick's mother. Since early morning she had sat in almost the same position, plying her needle unceasingly, and when her day's work is done she will have barely earned a shilling. Since morning Dick had been in the streets, ready to turn his hand to anything, or earn a penny by any honest means.

"Well, Dick, my boy," she said, looking up from her work with a smile, "you are late to-night."

"Ay, mother," he answered, going up to her and kissing her. "I ain't had very good luck, an' I waited for anything as might turn up, an' then I waited to help a little gal as tumbled down in the street, an'—"

"I'm not complainin'," broke in the mother, "an' I'm glad you helped the little girl. You'll never lose anything by bein' kind, but it's quite time we had our bit of supper an' got to bed."

"Well, I'll be glad of some'at to eat, anyhow," said Dick, "for I'm near clemmed."

"Then blow the fire a bit while I get the herrin'," said the mother; and soon after the herring was sputtering on the coals, and Dick was smacking his lips over the savoury smell.

There was very little said during the meal, for neither mother nor son was in the mood for conversation. She was tired, and sad, and anxious to forget her toil and pain and poverty, in sleep. He was full of thoughts of Fairy. If his mother had given him any encouragement to talk, he would have told her all about the little waif that he had protected; but she was evidently too tired to be troubled with the troubles of any one else, and he was not sorry to be quiet.

For long after he had crept into his poor bed he lay awake listening to the wind, and thinking of Fairy; and she, on Luther's big sofa, lay thinking of him, and wondering what the end of her adventure would be.

Almost as soon as it was day, he started for Luther's house. The old man was busy cooking his breakfast, and Fairy, looking as fresh and pretty as a spring flower, was watching his operations with evident interest.

"Had owt to eat, lad?" was Luther's greeting.

"Not yet," said Dick. "Mother's havin' a hextra nap this mornin'. She were fair beat last night."

"Well, never mind," said Luther, "there 's 'nough here

for three on us. So ye're welcome to a snack."

"Well," says Dick, with a broad grin, "I'm not such a fool as to say no to a good hinvitation, so I'll stop."

"I'm glad you's goin' to have breakfas' here," said Fairy. "It'll be fine together."

"Ay," said Dick; "an don't that bacon jist smell tip-top! Bother my buttons if one didn't ought to 'ave a piece of bread to eat wi' it."

"Now, look here," said Luther, when breakfast was over, "and hearken to what I'm a-goin' to say. I'm goin' out to make inquiries 'bout this little gal. You hear, Fairy?"

She nodded her head.

"I'm goin' to ferret it out, if there's sich a thing as doin' it, blamed if I don't; an' if that Mrs. Limber's a right to the gal, if she's a relation, or guardian, or owt of that sort, well, back the gal'll have to go. A nice mess I shall get into if I'm found out harbouring a gal as ought to be returned to her friends! There's been no wrong done yet, an' I ain't a-goin' to git into trouble for anybody if I knows it. Do ye understand?"

Both Dick and Fairy nodded their heads.

"Well, then, till I've ferreted out this business nobody must know the gal's here. Did anybody see yer come?"

"No, nobody" said Dick.

"So much the better," went on Luther. "But have you told yer mother?"

"No, she didn't give me the chance."

"Then don't tell her—don't tell anybody; keep dark till I've got to th' bottom of it. Now, Dick, thee be off 'bout thy business, and Fairy'll have to keep upstairs till I come back, and not even show her face at winder."

A few minutes later Fairy was alone, and Dick and

III

DICK'S GLUEPOT

BY DARK, OR A little after, Dick had succeeded in earning a shilling, an achievement he had never before accomplished, and, as a consequence, he was greatly elated. Ninepence he had earned during the early part of the day in sweeping the snow from people's doorsteps and garden paths; the other threepence was profit on the sale of evening papers. Besides this, a lady, taking compassion on his hungry looks, had given him a great piece of bread and cheese, which made him an excellent dinner; while another lady, touched by the sight of his rags, had given him an old suit of clothes that would serve him all the winter.

Dick felt that if he was not set up for life he was next door to it. In all his experience he had never done such a stroke of business. In his hand were twelve copper coins. What might they not represent! What vast possibilities might they not contain! One much-coveted and long-hoped-for treasure, at least, was within his reach, and should be his before he slept. That treasure was a gluepot. He knew where there was one that could be purchased for fivepence—second-hand, it is true, but almost as good as new.

So off he started, when his last paper had been disposed of, for the lumber-shop where the gluepot was to be had. He was in a fever of fear lest it should have been sold. No, thank goodness! it was in the window still, and Dick marched boldly into the shop.

"What'll yer take for that owd gluepot there?" he asked of the woman in charge of the shop.

Without speaking she unhooked it and looked at the bottom, and then at Dick.

"Well, what'll yer take for 't?" he demanded.

"Fivepence," was the answer.

"Hope ye'll get it, I reckon; but I'll give yer threepence for 't."

"You hope *you'll* get it, I reckon," she snapped, proceeding to hang it up again.

"Bother yer buttons!" he ejaculated, "ye needn't be in sich a tearing hurry. Let's look at it."

"Well," he said, after examining it carefully for some time, "I'll tell yer what I'll do: I'll give yer fourpence for it. There, now, I can't afford no more."

There was considerable objection to this at first, but Dick persevered, and at last walked off with his long-coveted treasure in triumph.

His next purchase was twopennyworth of glue, and then he turned his face towards home, eager to communicate to his mother his good fortune; and yet, eager as he was, he could not resist the impulse that led him round by Luther's house, for he was burning to know the fate of Fairy. There was no light however, in Luther's window, and when he tried the door he found it fast, so with a sigh he turned away, and once more directed his steps towards Tinker's Row.

"Now, mother, I've made my fortin at last," was his greeting; and the tired woman looked up from her work with a wan smile, but did not reply.

"I see yer don't believe it," went on Dick, "but look at these 'ere togs; an' better'n all the togs in the world,

24

I've got the gluepot at last."

"I'm afraid you've been spendin' yer money foolishly," sighed the mother.

"Not a bit of it," said Dick. "Wi' perseverance, cork, an' glue I'm goin' to make my fortin,"

"My poor boy, you'll find out that fortins are not so easily made. There's no chance i' this world for folks as is poor, so you'd better be content to struggle on as you are." And Mrs. Dugdale went on again with her sewing.

Nothing discouraged, however, Dick set his gluepot on the fire and commenced operations. His idea was to model a church with bits of cork glued together. He had seen such a model once in a shop window under a glass case, and was told that the price of it was five pounds.

"Moses, what a fortin!" was his exclamation. And though he never hoped or expected that he could accomplish anything half so perfect, yet if he could make a toy church, and get five shillings for it, it would be a great thing.

A great thing! Who could tell how great? It would be a new start in life, with boundless possibilities on ahead. Once started, what might it not lead to? Dick had only to close his eyes, and wonderful visions floated before him. But, alas! alas! where was he to get the gluepot? For months and months he had been gathering up bits of cork in dust-heaps and in the sweepings of warehouses, and these he had cut into shape with an old pocket-knife that was once his father's, but so far all his efforts had been fruitless for lack of glue. "If I'd on'y a gluepot," he had sighed a hundred times over, "there'd be a chance for a chap—but there, it won't come by worriting."

It may sound prosaic that all Dick's dreams of fame and fortune should be associated with anything so humble and mean as a gluepot, but it is quite true nevertheless. *That* with him was to be the magic wand that should change his rags into scarlet and fine linen, that should transmute the base metal of earth into shining gold. It was his last wish ere he dropped asleep at night, his first when he awoke in the morning, "If I on'y had a gluepot."

Now, however, his dream was realized. He had purchased the long-coveted treasure with his own money, and felt justified in the transaction. While he had earned only threepence or fourpence in a day, he felt duty bound to bring it all home to his mother. But "circumstances alter cases." Having earned a whole shilling, there was no longer any reason why he should deny himself; and at last before his eyes was the melted glue, and the church rising into shape.

That was the proudest evening of Dick's life. So happy was he, and so completely absorbed in his work, that he forgot the flight of time—forgot even Fairy, who, even then, perhaps, was sitting all alone, anxiously waiting to know her fate.

The frugal supper was placed on the table at last, but Dick had not noticed his mother getting it ready; he had eyes for nothing but the cork and glue; he never felt the gnawings of hunger. The longer he worked the more rapidly the visions passed before his eyes, and the more beautiful they became. The gluepot had become a magic wand already. Even now the poverty-stricken cottage had given place to a beautiful mansion, and in his imagination he was dwelling amid affluence and beauty.

His mother's sad, almost querulous voice dissipated his airy castles at length.

"I want no supper," he said.

"You silly lad," she answered. "Come at once."

Very reluctantly Dick obeyed, and bolted his supper in silence, then turned to his work again.

"No, no," said his mother; "I'm going to have no more of that nonsense to-night. Do you know what time it is?"

"It's not nonsense, mother," he said, without heeding her question; "an' you'll say so yet."

"Well, well, it's bed-time, anyhow," she said. "It's after ten o'clock."

"After ten?" he questioned in a tone of surprise.

"Ay," she said. "I'd no idea 't was so late till I got up to git supper ready."

But he did not heed what she was saying. He was thinking of Fairy. What had become of the little waif? he wondered. Here he had been all the evening, selfishly enjoying himself, and forgetting the child he had promised to defend. Perhaps Luther had already taken her back to Mrs. Limber; and if so, he should never see her face again. And what would she think of him, leaving her to her fate in that way, when he had vowed in her hearing that Mrs. Limber should never get hold of her again if he could help it? Poor Dick was quite distressed. If it had been an hour earlier—half-past nine instead of half-past ten—he would still have ventured on paying a visit to Luther; but it was too late now. The old man was such an early bird that it would be folly to go at this hour.

Dick's sleep was very much troubled that night, and his dreams considerably mixed. Now he was flying across the country in a wild chase after Mrs. Limber, who had got possession of Fairy, and was going to subject her to unheard-of tortures; and now, as a gallant gentleman, he was floundering in a lake of liquid glue, and hopelessly struggling to save Fairy, who was drowning in the same; now Fairy had been changed into cork, and he was fixing her in a niche in a great tower he was building; and now she had fallen to pieces, and he was glueing her together again, and finding infinite difficulty in getting the pieces to fit.

Dick was thankful when at last the night was over, and the grey dawn of the clear December day began to struggle through the grimy window. Slipping quietly out of bed, he proceeded to dress himself in the clothes that had been given him the day before.

"It's a odd lot, any way," was his reflection. "An' the weskit fits me a mite too much. But what's the odds? I'll be as warm as Nebichadneezer, King o' the Jews, wi' his cast-iron stockin's an' timber shoes." And with this reflection he lifted the door-latch quietly and passed swiftly into the street.

"Owd Luther's sure to be up," was his reflection. "He allers goes in for the top o' the mornin'. But I do hope he ain't a-given up the little gal."

It did not take him many minutes to reach Luther's dwelling, but a glance at the shuttered window showed him that the old man was not stirring yet.

"Mighty queer," said Dick to himself, scratching his head. "I can't make it up no road. The owd bloke's allers stirring wi' the first peep o' th' mornin'. There's summat i' th' wind, I fear."

Half an hour later Dick returned again, but the shutter had not been taken down from the window, and the door was still locked.

What could it mean? There was a mystery somewhere that he could not unravel; and after loitering in the street for what seemed to him the best part of an hour, he reluctantly, and with a heavy heart, turned away, and bent his steps towards the city.

IV

LOST, STOLEN, OR STRAYED

TO FAIRY, THAT FIRST day in Luther's house was an intensely trying one. Hour after hour she sat alone in the silent house waiting for Luther's return, and yet almost dreading his coming. She could not quite understand the old man yet, and did not seem at all certain whether to regard him as a friend or a foe.

The little she had seen of him had perplexed her greatly. One moment he would smile upon her, the next he would frown. Now he would speak in tones that were gentle and tender, and now, as if to remove any impression of gentleness, he would speak in tones that were sharp and stern.

That he meant to do what he considered right there could be no doubt. But what might seem right to him might be the cruellest wrong to her. Should she wait there for his return, or should she slip quietly out of the house and make off, and trust to chance, or to that Providence that old Mr. Limber sometimes had spoken to her about when his vixen wife was out of the way?

It seemed a difficult question for her to decide. It was awfully lonely sitting in that strange house with no one to speak to, and debarred even the small comfort of looking out of the window. It was scarcely better than being exposed to Mrs. Limber's fury, and very likely if she waited till Luther's return, he would take her back to the old life from which she had tried to escape, and which would be worse to her than death.

On the other hand, if she stole off while Luther was out she would forfeit Dick's friendship, and perhaps not effect her escape after all. For where was she to go to, and how was she to get food and a place to sleep in? And if the police found her wandering about, they would be certain to take her back to Mrs. Limber, as they had done before.

She was not quite six, and little for her age, but she was shrewd beyond her years. The wandering life she had led almost since she could remember had quickened all her faculties, and made her old in speech and thought.

She decided, after a while, to stay where she was, and risk the consequences.

Soon after dark Luther came in without a word, and set to work at once to get the supper ready. Poor little Fairy was in an agony of fear, and eagerly scanned his face, if by that means she could learn the result of his quest. But Luther's rugged face was not easy to read, and with a sigh that was almost a sob she coiled herself up in the corner of the sofa and waited till he should speak. She longed to break the silence herself, yet did not dare. This strange man was an object of fear to her yet.

"You must be hunger'd, little gal," he said to her when the meal was ready.

"No, not very much," was the timid answer, and then the meal proceeded in silence.

After supper he betook himself to his easy chair, and lighted his pipe, and Fairy watched him from the corner of the sofa without a word.

"I ain't found out nothing yet," he said at length. "So yer safe for another night, little gal."

Fairy did not speak. Her little heart was too full just

then, but she slipped off the sofa and came and stood beside his chair, and began, in a timid fearful way, to smooth his hard wrinkled hand with her little white palm.

He did not notice her for awhile, but went on smoking as usual. At length he looked up at her with a start. He had felt a hot scalding tear fall upon his hand, and it seemed to touch him to the quick.

"Don't cry, little gal," he said huskily. "I won't harm yer, if I knows it. I'd rather do ye good."

She began to cry in earnest now. Hiding her face in his shoulder, she sobbed as though her heart were breaking. All the day's pent-up dread and anxiety and grief found vent now in easeful tears, and the more he tried to soothe her the more she sobbed.

Luther got quite distressed at length. He knew nothing about children or their ways, and he was utterly at a loss to account for such violent weeping.

"Are you so very miserable, Fairy?" he said, smoothing her bright silken hair with his horny hand.

"Oh, no," she said between her sobs; "but I've been so lonely all the day, an' I can't help it now you've come."

"And ye're glad I'm comed home, are ye?" he said.

"Oh, yes, very glad, now I know you are not going to take me back to Mrs. Limber."

"Not to-night, that is," he answered, taking her up in his arms.

And now Fairy's last fear vanished. She felt somehow that Luther was her friend now, and was afraid of him no longer.

"I'm not 'fraid of yer a bit now, Mr. Luther," she said at length, nestling closer to him.

"No?" he said, in a questioning tone. And then silence fell between them.

31

Into Luther's dim eyes there came a far-away look, as though the old man's thoughts were back in the distant years—in the green and sunny paths of youth. He forgot his pipe in his dreams of what might have been. This fair young head nestled against his breast had awakened longings that never could be realized now. How lonely his life had been! How empty of all the things that make life sweet! If—if—oh, that "If"! And yet he could but think if little children had grown around his kneee, and *she* of other years—but who was sleeping in the green grave now—had shared his lot, he had been a better man to-day, and might not have lost his faith in man and God as now was the case.

Oh, blessed children! Tiresome as ye are sometimes, yet surely are ye ministers of God to weary men. How dark would home be without the patter of your little feet! And how lonely life, without your noisy laughter and happy songs!

When Luther got back from his dreams he found that his pipe was out, and Fairy was fast asleep in his arms; so he laid her gently on the sofa, and tucked her in warm for the night, and then betook himself to rest. But he did not sleep for many an hour. Emotions had been stirred that night that had lain dormant for many years. Memories of the past had been awakened, and would not be lulled to sleep agin. One sentence kept ringing in his ears all the while,—

"And a little child shall lead them."

Where had he seen these words? What did they mean? What reference could they have to himself? Had he gone astray, and was this little child sent to lead him right?

Bah! He remembered where the words were to be found now. He had read them in the Bible—a book he had long since discarded as an idle tale. They had some connection with lions and bears. But what was that to him? He didn't believe in the Bible—so he said: did not believe in God or devil, hell or heaven: had no faith in men or angels. And yet, for all that, the words haunted him, and they brought to his memory other words from the same old Book. Then an old question came back to him that he thought he had settled thirty years before: "Was there a Providence after all?" Had this child come to him by mere chance? Was it simply an event in the chapter of accidents? Or was there some arrangement in the plan of the child's life and of his?

He was vexed with himself for allowing such a question to trouble him. He called himself "a Freethinker," but that did not mean that he was free to think or believe anything. Oh, no! A Freethinker is only allowed to think along the Freethinker's lines, and believe the Freethinker's creed. If a Freethinker—so called—should happen to think that there may be a Providence, or to believe in an Omnipotent God, he may as well change his sect and his title first as last.

Luther was astonished at himself that he should actually be found debating a question that his fraternity had relegated to the limbo of exploded superstitions. Certainly he was not so settled in his belief as he had imagined.

He fell asleep, however, at length, and with the first glimmer of dawn he was off again, locking the door behind him. He had told Fairy that he would be back as soon as possible, and with that she was fain to be content. She heard someone try the door a little later, and, guessing it was Dick, called out for him to come round to the back; but he did not hear her, and so went away troubled, as we have seen.

Soon after noon Luther came back flushed and excited.

"I shall have to give yer up, little gal, I fear," he said.

"Give me up?" she asked, in a questioning tone. "What do yer mean, Mr. Luther?"

"I mean I shall have to hand ye over to Mrs. Limber," he said.

"Oh, no, no, Mr. Luther!" she said, "Ye'll never do that, will ye? Oh, say ye'll never do that! Oh, Mr. Luther, she'd kill me if she got me back again!" And the child crouched at his feet in an agony of terror.

"Well, listen to this," said Luther, and he pulled a handbill out of his pocket and began to read:—

" 'Lost, stolen, or strayed, a little girl of about six years of age, called Fairy, small for her years, and exceedingly intelligent. When last seen was dressed in a mixture of calico and tulle, set off by pink ribbon. Had on pink and white stockings, and white kid boots. Any one giving such information at the Police Station, Cross Street, as shall lead to her recovery shall be handsomely rewarded by her distracted parents.'

"It's those last words as settles the matter," said Luther, after a pause. "Distracted parents! If they're yer parents, ye'll have to go back."

"But they're not my parents," said Fairy indignantly; "an' I'll never go back!"

"You can't prove it, my child," said Luther kindly, "nor I either; that's where the pinch comes in."

"But I'll run away from here," said Fairy.

"And the police 'ud pick ye up in five minutes," said Luther. "No, my child, there's no help for it, as I can see. Ye'll have to go back."

Poor little Fairy felt that these words were true, and buried her face in the sofa in an agony of grief.

V

LUTHER AS A PRIVATE DETECTIVE

"IT'S VERY STRANGE," THOUGHT Luther, as he sat on the sofa by the sobbing child, stroking her glossy hair, "very strange how this little gal's got hold of my heart. She's like a bit of sunshine in this old house, an' it sadly goes agin the grain to send her back to that woman to be kicked an' abused. I shall be always thinkin' about her, ay, an' pityin' her too. I wish something could be done for the little lass to save her from sich a life.

"Come, come, little gal," he said at length, "don't cry any more. I'll not send ye back to-night. I'll take a bit more time to think it over, any way."

"Oh, you good Mr. Luther!" said the child impulsively; and before the old man was aware the little arms were around his neck, and the child's soft face pressed close to his.

Later in the day Dick came in, bringing his model church, and Luther left the two to play together, while he smoked in silence by the fireside. Dick was delighted beyond bounds at finding Fairy still with the old man.

"Is he goin' to send yer away?" Dick whispered to her at length.

"I's 'fraid so," she answered, her eyes filling. "But he ain't sure. He's goin' to think 'bout it till mornin'."

"Oh, then don't trouble," said Dick encouragingly, "He's mighty knowin', an' if there's a hole out o' the

35

bizness anywheres, he's sartin to find it."

Fairy was delighted with Dick's church, but Luther did not condescend to notice it. He was too busy with his own thoughts—too anxious about Fairy.

Luther scarcely slept a wink that night, but before morning he had formed a daring resolution and directly after breakfast set off to execute it.

Fairy hardly recognized Luther in his Sunday best clothes, his hands encased in brown kid gloves, and a respectable wideawake hat upon his head.

"Why, Mr. Luther," she said, with her usual frankness, "you look like a gentleman."

"Keep dark, little gal, till I come back," he said. and he went out, locking the door behind him. At the police station he found out Mrs. Limber's where-abouts, and then made straight for the "fair-ground." There were not many caravans about, so he easily discovered which belonged to the Limbers. Mrs. Limber was washing the steps when he came up. She was a coarse hard-featured woman of some five-and-forty years of age.

"You are Mrs. Limber, I presume?" said Luther, speaking as pompously as possible, and using his very best English.

"Yah, I be," she answered. "An' who are yow?"

"Do not talk so loud, my good woman," said Luther. "I'm come about the little gal you've lost."

"An' what 'ave yow to do wi' her?" she snarled.

"Well," he said, "if you must know, I'm a private detective." Our readers will think he was a *very* private one.

"Oh, indeed," said the woman, rather taken aback, and dropping her voice to a whisper. "I thowt detectives were allers younger men."

36

"I'm a private detective."

"There you are mistaken," he said. "Age brings experience, and experience makes fools wise. But now about the gal, for men of our class have no time to waste. You say her name is Fairy. Fairy what?"

"Dunno," said Mrs. Limber, taken off her guard. "There, there, what a fool I be! Fairy Limber, in course."

"Come, come, Mrs. Limber, this won't do. We may as well fling up the case if we can't get truthful answers. What's the child's surname?"

"Limber," snarled the woman.

"Woman," said Luther sternly, "do you take us detectives to be fools? You have no children, you know— never had—so what's the use o' lying?"

"How'd you get to know that?"

"How?" said Luther scornfully. "We get to know everything. You wonder, I suppose, how I got to know you stole the child?"

This was a random shot of Luther's, but it took immensely. The woman turned deadly pale, and seemed for a moment ready to fall.

"Now, look here," said Luther, following up his advantage. "I'm not so young as I once were, and don't feel so disposed to be hard on folks as I used to do. We've found the child, and got her safe in a private asylum. But we've found out also she's not your child, you're no relation of hers—have no claim to her. In a court of law it 'ud go hard with you. However, we feel disposed to deal easy with you. We give you three hours' grace. If you're not cleared out by then you'll have to take the consequences. That's all I've got to say, Mrs. Limber. Good mornin'."

Mrs. Limber by this time was completely cowed. Luther had played his part splendidly. From a little distance—keeping well out of sight—he watched the effect of his words, and had the satisfaction of seeing—in less than an hour—the van, tents, and all the show trappings on the move.

"Blest if that ain't a caution," he chuckled to himself, as he turned his face homewards. "An' won't the little gal be set up, that's all?"

At length he stopped short in the street. "Hang me if I know what I'm to do wi' her now I've got her," he said to himself. "New clothes 'll have to be got for her, an' a bed, an' what else goodness knows—I don't."

He soon found out, however, what was wanted and from that day he seemed a changed man. He never forgot the hugging he received when he got home, nor the happy, thankful tears little Fairy shed.

"Oh, Mr. Luther, I do love yer!" she said, kissing him again and again; and that evening, as he sat in his easy chair with Fairy on his knee, there came back to him long-forgotten words, that haunted him all through the evening, and weaved themselves into his dreams when he slept: "Inasmuch as ye have done it unto one of the least of these my little ones, ye have done it unto me."

Strange, how this little waif that he had befriended brought back to him memories of the past, and stirred his heart with emotions deep and strange. Strange how words that best expressed his thoughts and feelings were to be found in that discarded book the Bible. Strange, too, that her presence continually made him think of things that did not belong to the physical realm, but were in their very nature spiritual, and because spiritual, perhaps eternal.

Luther thought it best that his neighbours should not know of Fairy's presence for another week, and in the meanwhile it got bruited abroad amongst them that "Owd Luther Cob were goin' to have some relation's orphan gal to live wi' 'im." So that when Fairy at length made her appearance in Luther's shop her presence occasioned no surprise.

"I tell yer she's an amazin' 'andy little critter," said Luther one day, in reply to some remark about her being a great trouble, "and ain't a bit o' trouble. She looks arter the house like a little woman, and dusts and shines the things so, till I don't know 'em sca'ce."

Luther seemed to grow almost young again under Fairy's influence. Life to him had a new meaning, ay, and a new responsibility. He had something to live for now. His day's toil grew light with Fairy prattling around him, and his evening's leisure was infinitely sweeter, because she was nigh. The better part of his nature had never sprung into life, nor blossomed into beauty, for lack of sunshine. But now the sunshine had come, and that soul of gentleness and kindness that had lain dormant so long began to awake into life, and out of the hard crust of his former life a new man was coming forth.

"I thinks it were God as brought me here, don't you, Mr. Luther?" Fairy said to him one evening when they were sitting alone.

Luther almost started from his seat. It was the very question that he at that moment was debating, almost unconsciously, with himself.

"What put that into your head, Fairy?" Luther said at length.

"I were thinkin' o' Mr. Limber," she said. "He used to say sometimes as 'ow the Great God 'ud make things right for us if we were good."

Luther made no reply to this. He had no reply to make.

He felt it would be cruel to shake the child's faith with his own doubts. He did not know then that his doubts were not so strong as her faith, but he found it out afterwards.

"I wish I were twenty year younger," Luther said to himself one evening, while smoking leisurely in his easy chair. "I seem to have a bit o' interest in life now, an' summat to live for."

Suddenly he started up, as though some one had spoken to him.

"He that findeth his life shall lose it, and he that loseth his life for my sake shall find it."

"Were that you speakin', Fairy?" he asked.

"No," she answered.

"Nor you, Dick?"

"No, we were neither on us speaking. We're too busy over th' new church," Dick replied.

"Queer!" said Luther to himself, sitting down again. "Mighty queer how these things do flash through one's brain, like. Seems to be a great deal of truth in that Book too, if one had only eyes to see it. Here I've been findin' my life all my life, an' missin' it all th' while; an' now, d'rectly I begins to lose my life as it were for this little gal, I begins to find it. I'll have a crack at that Book again some o' these days, for I were but a young man when I flinged it up; an' there seems a good bit o' what our chaps calls philosophy in it, after all."

Luther's reflections were interrupted at this point by a question from Fairy.

"Uncle Luther," she said, "what is churches for?"

"For parsons to preach in, an' folks to sit an' listen," he answered.

"What's to preach?" she asked.

"Oh, talk to folks."

"What do they talk to 'em about?"

"Oh, lots o' things."

"But what things?" Fairy persisted.

"Why, 'bout Jesus Christ, an' God, an' their sins, and heaven, an' them things."

"Oh," said Fairy reflectively, while Luther was started on a new train of thought, which he pursued far on into the night.

And so unconsciously the child was leading the man into new paths, and unconsciously he was following.

VI

GATHERING CLOUDS

ARCHITECTURALLY SPEAKING, DICK'S FIRST effort at church-building was a failure. When Luther at length condescended to notice it, he laughed immoderately.

"What yer call it?" he said.

"Why, a church, to be sure," said Dick, ruefully.

"Then you'd better write on a label, '*This is a Church,*' an' stick it on to the bottom," said Luther, "or nobody 'll never know."

"It ain't so bad's that, I'm sartin," said Dick, with tears in his eyes.

"But what's it for?" said Luther, without a touch of pity.

"For folks to buy, to be sure," said Dick.

"Buy?" said Luther. "Why, folks no more wants a thing like that than a toad wants side-pockets! Why, boy, it's neither wittles not drink, ornament nor use; so what's the good on it?"

But here Fairy came to the rescue. "It's too bad to larf at Dick so, when he's tried so hard," she said. "An I'm sure it's very nice."

Luther relented after that. "Well, well, boy," he said, "as a ornament it ain't no account, that's sartin; but p'r'aps it might be made useful, after all."

"Which way?" said Dick, brightening up.

"Well, come again to-morrow evenin', an' I'll get some catgut by then, and we'll see if we can't make a

43

weather-glass on it."

"A weather-glass!" said Dick, in surprise: "which way?" While Fairy looked as curious as Dick, though she said nothing.

"Well," said Luther, "some sorts o' catgut shrinks up or swells out accordin' as the weather's wet or dry, don't ye see? An' so we can fix it so as a sodger can come up on top o' th' tower when it's wet, an' a gal come out o' th' church door when it's dry. That'll be a new kind o' dodge, an' 'll take amazin' with country folks, I'm thinkin', and old Billy Beel as goes round buying rags'll be able to sell any amount."

This prediction of Luther's proved to be correct.

Billy Beel parted with Dick's first church and weather-glass combined for eighteen pence in hard cash and a shillingsworth of rags and bones; and so much was it admired in the village, that Billy got orders for a dozen more, and during the next fortnight there was a general hunt for rags, in order to pay for the novel toy when Billy should come round again.

When Dick received two silver shillings from Billy, and an order for twelve church weather-glasses at two bob apiece," he felt that all the bright and beautiful dreams of his life had come true at last.

"Oh, mother!" he cried, flinging open the door, and nearly frightening the poor woman out of her wits, "I'm a gent at last! I've made my fortin, as I told yer I should! Hurrah! I'm fit to burst!" And Dick described a cart-wheel revolution round the little apartment to save himself from such a disaster; while old Mrs. Podger, who lived in the room above, hurried downstairs to learn the cause of such commotion. "Book here, Mrs. Podger," said Dick, flinging up the two shillings and catching them in his hands, "talk about riches! An' this are only the beginnin'. There's twenty-four more on 'em to come. Hurrah! hurrah! I'll bust right up unless I shout!"

Dicks' mother smiled feebly at the lad's enthusiasm. She was too weary, too weak, too near the bound of time to take much interest in anything. She kissed him affectionately when he had cooled down a little, and called him a good lad; then she went on with her work. Perhaps she knew she could not do very much more, and so was eager to get done. She was employed by a large wholesale outfitting establishement in making articles at so much per dozen, and find her own needles and thread. They were cruel, *wicked* terms. People who are so eager to purchase *cheap* ready-made articles of apparel do not always know where they are made, or how. Perhaps it would be well sometimes if they did.

"I cannot bear the smell of the glue—it makes me sick," Dick's mother said to him the following day; and Dick had to give up his work, and go in search of Luther for advice.

"Oh, ye needn't trouble on that score," said the old man, kindly. "My shop's big enough for both, and will serve for show-room as well. So bring your traps here, my lad, an' work'll be all t' sweeter for company."

So Dick gave up going into the streets to earn his bread —gave up sweeping doorsteps, carrying bundles, and selling newspapers—and settled down as toy-maker in right good earnest, feeling that he had now found the proper business of his life. Nobody had ever dreamed that Dick was the genius that he afterwards proved himself to be. He was always clever with his pocket-knife in carving little things, but no one thought anything of that. But now that the opportunity was given, and his genius had room in which to develop itself, the latent powers of the lad

45

sprang into life as it were, and people wondered at the *variety* of toys which he planned and manufactured.

It was well that he was now able to earn a respectable sum week by week, for his mother fell ill directly after, or, more correctly, she became so much worse that she could work no longer, and so Dick had to maintain both himself and her.

In those dark days of sickness and anxiety, old Mrs. Podger, who occupied the second floor, proved herself to be a real friend. She waited upon the sick woman with unremitting care and attention, asking for no pay or thanks—glad only, it seemed, that she was allowed to render help.

But behind this there was a secret reason, which we must hasten to explain. Years before, when she used to go out with a little basket of tapes and pins—a respectable method of begging—she found she could always do best if she had a child in her arms. A child's sunny smile or tearful eyes would often win a penny or a crust, where, otherwise, the door would be slammed in her face.

Now in those days Mrs. Dugdale had a little girl—born about a month after her husband's death—and it was a relief to her sometimes to let Mrs. Podger take the child for a day, for she knew the woman had a kind heart, and would exercise the greatest care.

When little Florence—or Florrie as they called her—was about fifteen months old, poor Mrs. Dugdale was smitten down with rheumatic fever, and in those days she felt truly thankful to Mrs. Podger for taking charge of the child day after day.

One day, however, she returned without the child. She was in a state of the wildest grief imaginable. Her story was that she went into a public house to have a pint

46

of beer; that she set the child down on a chair while she found her purse and drank the beer. There were many people before the counter—she said—and she stood talking for a few minutes—she could not say how many—with her back towards the child. When, however, she turned round, the child was gone. No one had seen the child run away; no one had seen any person take her; hence what had become of her was a mystery. The streets were searched in all directions, inquiries were instituted far and wide, but all without avail. Poor Mrs. Dugdale was heartbroken, and Mrs. Podger nearly went off her head.

About a fornight later the body of a child was found in the canal, but almost unrecognizable. Poor Mrs. Dugdale was still unable to leave her bed, so Mrs. Podger went to view the body.

"It's little Florrie, sure enough," she said, on her return. "The hair's hers; I could swear to the hair. I never seen a child 'ave hair like it but Florrie, and I've cut off a lock an' brought it for you to see. Tender little darlin', I wish it wur me as was drownded instead." And the woman sat down and burst into a flood of tears.

Mrs. Dugdale looked at the lock of hair long and earnestly, and then she too began to cry.

"Oh, my darlin,' my darlin'!" she wailed. And poor Mrs. Podger had no word of comfort to give. But ever after that she felt she could never do enough for the woman who—through her—had been so terribly stricken.

As the days passed on, Mrs. Dugdale got worse instead of better, and when at length the parish doctor came, he gave no hope. Poor woman! she had worked herself to death to save her life.

Dick had seen his mother ill so many times that he never though of her dying. He knew that she was worn out with hard work, and thought that a week or two of rest in bed would set her up again; and in his heart he resolved that she should never work so hard again as she had been in the habit of doing.

"I can 'arn enough for both on us now," he said to himself, somewhat proudly; "an' mother shall take it easy for the rest o' her life."

Now and then Fairy went in to see Mrs. Dugdale, but not very often, for the poor woman was unable to bear the least excitement. She took a wonderful fancy to Fairy, however, and stroked the child's silken hair with her wasted hand, in a manner that was quite pathetic in its tenderness. Perhaps she thought of her own little child, that had been so cruelly taken from her, and who would have been about Fairy's age had she lived.

So the dark days of that dreary winter passed on, and Mrs. Dugdale got gradually worse. Dick worked early and late to get little delicacies to tempt her appetite, and wondered how it was that, having rested so long, she was not completely rested and able to get about again.

She knew herself she would never get better, and one Saturday evening—feeling, perhaps, that the end was drawing nigh—she called Dick to her bedside, and, kissing him tenderly, said to him,—

"I shall soon be gone from you now, my child."

For a moment he looked at her in utter bewilderment, then all the truth burst upon him, and hiding his face in the beclothes, he began to cry.

"No, no, my boy, do not cry," she said. "It is best as it is. But I have something I want to say to you to-night, something that has been upon my mind all the day, an' has been growin' there for days. Now dry your eyes, my child, an' listen."

VII

"MISSING"

"I THINK IT MUST ha' been little Fairy Cob," she said—speaking in a low tone of voice—"that's made me think so much about it. She's a purty little creature. I never took so to a strange child before; but all my heart goes out to that little gal, somehow. P'r'aps it's because little Florrie 'ud ha' been just like her if she 'ad lived." And the poor woman sighed, and was silent for a moment or two. Then she went on again,—

"P'r'aps it's very foolish on me to think anything 'bout it, but yer mind, Dick, I was ill with the rheumatiz, an' couldn't go mysel'. Mrs. Podger brought back a lock o' her hair, an' she seemed quite sartin as 't was little Florrie's body. I daresay it were, but there was nothin' but the hair to swear by; 'an she *might* ha' been mistaken. If she could only ha' seen the marks—"

"What marks?" said Dick quickly.

"That's just what I were a-goin' to tell yer. So that if ye ever hear anything, or see anything in the papers 'bout a little gal bein' found wi' those marks—But there, there, it's foolish, I daresay."

"But you ain't told me what marks," persisted Dick.

"Oh, well," sighed the poor woman, "little Florrie had a mark on her left arm, just below the shoulder, for all the world like a bunch of purple grapes, an' on her left foot was a mark made by a burn. Poor little gal! she had a bad foot, too! But when it healed, it left a mark just like a button—a flat, double-eyed button. Poor little gal! I never could make out 'ow she got into the canal."

"It were mighty queer," said Dick; "but it ain't no use frettin' bout it now, mother. She's better off, likely."

"Oh, yes! she's better off. She's gone to the good place an' p'r'aps I'll see her again. I ain't been able to go to church nor chapel for many years; but I think, for all that, the good Lord'll let me in."

Dick made no reply to this. He had no reply to make.

"Ye've always been a good boy, Dick," she went on at length, her eyes growing moist while she spoke—"always a good boy. I hope ye'll never grow bad—"

But here a fit of coughing came on, and she was able to say no more for several minutes.

"I'd like to see Fairy in the mornin', Dick," she gasped at length. And then the cough came on again.

"Ye mun talk no more to-night," said Mrs. Podger, coming into the room. "An' it's time, Dick, thee were in thy bed."

An hour later all three were fast asleep, and the silence was unbroken save for the ticking of the old Dutch clock. And then there came into the room a messenger whom no one saw or heard; but he touched the heart of the sleeping woman, and it grew gently still. There was no struggle—scarcely a sigh. The wheels of life had been revolving slowly for many a day, and still the pace slackened as the hours went on, until, without a wrench or jar, they quietly stopped. She sleeping—died—nor heard the summons, nor felt the chill. She lay her down and slept, and awoke to other scenes and to a better life.

It was pitiful to see Dick's grief in the morning, when she would not heed his call. He could not, *would* not, believe that she was dead. He tried at length to open her death-sealed eyes; then started back in affright, and rushed out of the house to call Luther. For a week he seemed almost demented. After the funeral Luther offered to share with him his bed-room, but he would not hear of it: while he could afford to keep the little room he would keep it—so he told the old man.

Mrs. Podger was glad for him to stay, and promised to take his mother's place all she could, and in this the old woman made good her promise. As the spring advanced Dick recovered his usual cheerfulness, and worked at his toys with a will. He never had very much money to spare, as he was always wanting new tools, and some of these were very expensive. Still he was paving the way—if slowly, yet surely—to future success. Luther was a constant help to him. Dick had the genius and Luther the experience, and so between them they managed well, while little Fairy supplied inspiration to both.

The long evenings they spent together were not only times of pleasure but of profit to all. Luther found them books and taught them to read, while they in turn plied him with questions that set him on trains of thought that proved a blessing to him in many ways.

The long-discarded Bible became a text-book in time, and Luther became a student of that Book of books, and found in it food for his hungry spirit and healing for his wounded heart, Not that he admitted this, even to himself. "He was still a 'freethinker,' " he said, "and read the Book to please the children;" and with this little fiction he was fain to be content. In truth he was afraid to inquire too closely into the matter, lest he should discover that his once much-boasted scepticism had taken flight. Indeed, he had a strong suspicion that this was so, and hence preferred to let things drift. He was very happy; at least, he was happier than he had been for forty years. Fairy was a constant source of interest and joy to him. It was a joy to anticipate her wants, a joy to plan some little surprise, a joy to answer her many questions.

So the days sped on on feet of down, and spring began to bloom into glorious summer. The evenings were now given to rambling in the parks and excursions into the country. Sometimes Luther accompanied Dick and Fairy; sometimes they went alone. It all depended on the distance.

These were the proudest hours of Dick's life, when he felt that he was Fairy's champion, and that it was his especial business to see that no harm befell her. Some of Dick's old companions got small courtesy when they tried to obtrude themselves upon his—and Fairy's—attention.

Once a big lad tried to pull Fairy's hair. His object was to tease Dick, and he quickly discovered that this was the easiest way of accomplishing his purpose.

"Now look 'ere," said Dick, "ye'll be gittin' me riled d'rectly. So ye'd better hook it."

"I shall hook it when I like," was the answer; for Dick had never been a fighting lad, and so his threats were very little feared.

"Then don't pull Fairy's hair again," Dick answered, "or I'll knock yer inter the middle o' next week."

"Oh, yer will, will yer?" said the lad squaring up. "Two ken play at that game. So ye'd better try it on."

"Pull Fairy's hair again, an' ye'll see if I don't try it on, an' feel it too."

"Ye thinks I's afeard, I s'pose?" said the lad, running up to Fairy, and giving her hair a vigorous tug. The next moment he saw more stars than Newton ever discovered. For Dick had pounced upon him with all the suddenness of a panther, and dealt him a blow between the eyes that fairly stunned him. He soon recovered himself, however, and returned the compliment, and then ensued a stand-up fight, much to the delight of a dozen or twenty lads that were soon on the scene.

The contest was short, sharp, and decisive, and Dick came off with flying colours in more senses than one. The prevailing colour, however, was crimson, and both combatants returned to their homes with banners flying and streamers gaily flaunting in the wind.

Dick's attempts to get into his clothes next morning were perfectly ludicrous. "Bother my buttons if I ain't got more pockets than pence!" he soliloquized, as, sitting on the side of the bed, he patiently endeavoured to find a way into his unmentionables, and only succeeded with every attempt in finding a way out of them.

Dick, however, was not much troubled at a few rags. It was what he had been used to ever since he could remember, and plenty of ventilation during summer-time, according to his idea, was rather a matter of thankfulness than of regret.

Dick's fight was not without its good results. Up to that time he had occasionally been called a coward, but he never was after. Nor did any lad attempt to molest Fairy again when Dick was about. "He's a reg'lar bruiser when 'is blood's up," said the lads to each other, and so prudently avoided giving him offence.

On Sundays Fairy and Dick visited all the churches and chapels within a mile of Tinker's Row. In this matter they certainly were not bigots. Their object, they informed Luther, "was to find out the place where they 'ad the best singin', and the chap as could talk the fastest, an' then to go there reg'lar."

It was great amusement to Luther to hear them discussing matters on their return. Sometimes it was the singing that was discussed, sometimes it was the sermon. Fairy, however, generally came out best in the discussion, for Dick would rather give up his opinion than give her pain. She was all the world to him now, since his mother was taken away. And no sacrifice he would consider too great if Fairy might be made happy thereby.

So the pleasant peaceful days sped on. In Luther's workshop there was laughter and singing all day long, for neither dreamt of evil, or saw the ominous cloud that was rising above the horizon and threatening to overspread all their sky.

It was a calm peaceful evening, early in September, that there came to Luther and Dick the first thought of evil. Fairy had gone down into the city on an errand for Luther, and had not returned.

"Fairy's been a long time, ain't she, Dick?" said Luther, looking up from his work.

"She's loiterin', lookin' at the winders, I spect," said Dick, with no thought of evil or danger.

For another half-hour the work went on in silence; then Luther threw down the shoe he had been mending.

"I wish the little gal was home, anyhow," he said. "I'm gettin' quite fidgety 'bout her."

"I don't think there's any cause," said Dick. "She's been out later nor this lots o' times."

"But she's been mor'n two hours away," said Luther; "an' it's quite dark."

"But she knows the way very well," said Dick, who was not disposed, as a rule, to go to meet trouble.

For another quarter of an hour there was silence. Then Luther donned his hat and went forth to meet her, while Dick, busy with his work, did not notice how time fled.

Luther did not return for fully an hour, and then he came alone.

"Ain't Fairy turned up?" was his first exclamation.

"No, said Dick, getting up quickly from his work. "Ain't ye found her?"

But Luther was silent. He was too agitated to speak. He had been to the shop where he had sent her, and discovered that early in the evening she had called and got the errand he had sent her for, and that she had then started at once for home.

"What's us to do?" said Dick, at length, seeing how agitated the old man was.

"Do, boy?" said Luther, in a hard unnatural voice. "I dunno what we's to do. I'm fair boggled. Maybe she's got run over. Don't believe it, though blamed if I do; she's too nimble for that. I fear she's been kidnapped."

"Kidnapped?" said Dick inquiringly.

"Ay, boy. She was a fortin to that woman Limber. Think o' that."

Dick did think of it for awhile, and then shook his head.

"No," he said; "I don't think that woman 'ud dare show up hereabouts. We'd better wait a bit longer. She may be turning up d'rectly."

So they waited in silence and in fear; waited until the streets grew silent and the evening deepened into night. Waited till they could wait no longer. Then they stared to their feet, and each asked the other, "What shall we do?"

VIII

A DISCOVERY

TO STAY LONGER IN the house was an impossibility, so they went out into the street, and stood for some time before the open door, watching and listening. The clocks all over the city had just sounded the hour of midnight, and Luther and Dick were looking dumbly and hopelessly at each other when they were startled by a footstep. For a moment hope brightened their faces, then as quickly vanished. The footsteps were heavy and slow.

"It's only a Bobby," said Dick ruefully.

Still the footsteps came nearer, till the heavy form of a policeman loomed into sight.

"He may ha' heard something," said Luther. "Anyhow there can be no harm in axing him."

"Ay, there ken be no 'arm," said Dick, in a tone that indicated that he thought there could neither be any good.

"If yer please," said Luther, advancing to meet the policeman, "we've lost a little gal, and we thought maybe ye might ha' heard summat about er'."

"Lost a little gal?" said the policeman, brightening up instantly. "When did it 'appen? where did it 'appen? and 'ow did it 'appen?" And he pulled out his note-book and pencil, and struck an attitude.

"Ye ain't a-heard nothin' 'bout her then?" said Luther, in a disappointed tone of voice.

"In course not," said the policeman. "How was we

goin' to 'ear anythink about 'er till we knowed she were lost? But if you'll favour me with all perticklers, we'll soon find out what's become o' her."

"P'r'aps ye'd better come inside a bit, then," said Luther, "for it's a longish story, an' I've got my own notion what's become o' her, though of course I may be mistaken."

"Very good," said the policeman. "Any suspicion o' yours'll 'ave due consideration." And he followed Luther into the house.

Here Luther, whether wisely or unwisely—he was not certain himself which—told the policeman all the story of Fairy from beginning to end.

"Humph," said the policeman, rubbing his chin and looking wise, "the case is more complicated than I at first supposed. Howsomever, you've hacted wise in bein' so circumstanshul. I think it not onlikely that your view is the kerrect one, in which case, supposin' the said Mrs. Limber, in the first person a hactin' on her own jurisdicshun, have wilfully and in her right mind, or by hagents hinstigated by the said Mrs. Limber, have knowin'ly detained or otherwise pervented, with or without vi'lence, and against her will and hinterests, to coax, persuade, or otherwise waylay in hopposition to all legal jewsamprudence, and by virtue of hacts known, unknown, or circumstanshul, have in the fust person of the said Mrs. Limber unlawfully kidnapped, detained, or caused to be hindered, detained, or kidnapped, in the case of one of the Queen's subjeks—"

"Oh, lor!" said Luther, at length, utterly aghast. "What in the name o' thunder are 'e a-drivin' at? for I'm blamed if I can make head or tail on it!"

"Excuse me," said the policeman, not in the least

abashed. "I forgot for a moment who I was a-talkin' to. Havin' so much to do wi' the law, we get into the way of usin' legal terms, you see. Well, as I were a-goin' to say, you seem to 'ave no more claim on the gal than Mrs. Limber, supposin' she's got hold o' her again."

"But I tell yer I 'ave," said Luther.

"How so?" said the policeman.

"Why, that Limber woman stole her, an' I didn't. She kept the little gal 'gainst her will, and I kept her 'cause she wanted to stay. That makes all the difference," said Luther triumphantly.

"Anyhow, we can test it," was the reply. "Meanwhile we may have to hadvertise a description o' her. Will yer furnish me wi' perticklers?"

"Hi, gladly," said Luther. And he gave a detailed account of her appearance and dress.

"There's nothin' you wish to hadd to this, I s'pose?" said the policeman at length, reading over the description.

"Well, I hardly know," said Luther. "I'm a-debatin' in my mind about it."

"About what?" asked the policeman.

"Well," said Luther, speaking slowly, "the little gal had a couple o' marks on her,"

At this, Dick, who had paid little heed to the conversation up to this point, suddenly sprang to his feet, and pressed eagerly forward to listen.

"On her left arm," went on Luther, "just below the shoulder, was a dark patch, for all the world like a bunch o' grapes, and on her left foot was a mark the size o' a shilling, that might ha' been a burn as had healed up."

"Oh, I know! I know!" said Dick, excitedly. "It's her, safe enough. Mother told me all 'bout it the night she died. Godness gracious! what a fool I've been never to think of it afore!"

"Think o' what afore?" said the policeman. "What does the boy mean?"

"Blamed if I know," said Luther. "What is it Dick? What is it yer drivin' at? Don't stand blinkin' there like a 'witched owl in the moonlight."

"It's Florrie," said Dick—"our Florrie—her as was drownded, or they thought as were. Don't you mind, Luther, how Mrs. Podger took 'er out an' lost her? Mother told me the night as she were took that she wern't sartin as how she were dead, an' she told me 'bout the marks as she could be swear'd to by."

"What does all this mean?" said the policeman. "I can't make head or tail on it yet."

By dint of a little cross-examination, however, Dick's meaning was made clear enough, and then poor old Mrs. Podger was called out of her bed to come and give her version of the case.

"I'd rather the little gal were livin' than be made Queen," said the old woman, trembling from head to foot with excitement.

"But I thought," said the policeman, "that you identified the body as was found in the canal?"

"Nobody could be sartin," said Mrs. Podger, "the body were that far gone. I thought it were her by the hair; there were no chance o' seein' the marks. But if Mr. Luther says as Fairy 'ad them marks, then it's Florrie, and she were never drowned at all, but stolen."

"I b'lieve mother had a kind o' feelin' as she were Florrie," said Dick, "for she axed me pertickler to let Fairy come in next mornin', but by mornin' she were gone, and that knocked it all out o' my noddle."

"Well, well," said the policeman, "all this puts a new

59

face on it. I will communicate perticklers to the chief detective at once." Saying which, he strode off to execute his mission.

Nothing, however, came of it. The detectives did their duty, no doubt. They questioned and cross-questioned Luther, Dick, and Mrs. Podger, until the trio were at their wits' end. They instituted inquiries far and wide; they sent telegrams to places distant and near; but not a single clue could they obtain of the missing child.

Luther was almost demented, while Dick was broken-hearted. For the first week they felt certain the police would discover her whereabouts. After that they grew less hopeful, and at last they yielded to despair.

Day after day Luther and Dick searched the great city in all directions, and each evening they returned weary and sad of heart. There was not a gipsy encampment for miles around, not a travelling show or circus, they did not visit. Every place likely and unlikely they searched, but all in vain. Neither Luther nor Dick thought of work. Time with them was no object, and what money they had was freely spent in prosecuting their search and when they returned at night they sat moody and silent, caring neither to eat or sleep.

Out of the house all the sunshine had gone, as though the sun of their life had been suddenly eclipsed; all music and laughter had ceased. On the willows they had hung their harps, and Dick at least mingled his bread with his tears. His grief would have been great under any circumstances, but the discovery that Fairy was his long-lost sister made it doubly so.

"On'y to think, Mr Luther," he said one evening in quaint paradox, the tears the while streaming down his cheeks, "on'y to think that I didn't find her till arter I'd lost her. Oh, dear! oh, dear!"

"Ay," said Luther, "it's mighty queer. I a'most thought once, boy, that there might ha' been a Providence as led her here, to lead me p'r'aps inter better ways, for that bit out o' the Bible kept ringin' in my head for days an' days—'And a little child shall lead 'em.' But I've got to give that up now: she can't lead me if she ain't here, that's sartin."

"P'r'aps she's took away 'cause yer wouldn't follow," said Dick, dolefully. "What's the use o' the Lord 'lowin' her to waste her time on yer, if ye wouldn't be led?"

"Blame it, boy, what's put that into thy noddle?" said Luther tartly.

"Dunno," said Dick; "it just comed in while ye were a-talkin'. But p'r'aps she's leadin' yer now without yer knowin'."

"Ay, sure enough she's leadin' us both a pretty chase, and without *her* knowin', most likely. Poor little gal! I wish I could get one sight o' her. I wouldn't lose her again, I warrant."

"Ay," said Dick, dolefully, "if wishin' 'ud bring her back she'd be here now."

There was little doubt in the mind of either of them what had become of the child. That Mrs. Limber had got hold of her again seemed a moral certainty, and as they thought of the life their little Fairy would have to lead, and the sufferings she would have to endure, their grief and indignation seemed more than they could bear.

For whole nights Dick would sometimes lie awake thinking about her, and in his vivid imagination he would picture her lying awake and calling in vain for help, suffering from blows and stripes, and with no one near to comfort—compelled to do what was hateful to her, and with no chance of deliverance; wishing to die, but with no chance even of that release. And when he slept, it was only to dream of Fairy. Often he would start up in his sleep, fancying he heard her calling, and sometimes the impression was so vivid that he would open the door and look out into the street, and call softly, "Fairy, Fairy." But no answer came to him out of the darkness, and with a sigh he would shut the door, and seek his lonely bed again.

It was no matter of surprise that Mrs. Limber should have discovered Fairy's whereabouts, for tramps are ever on the move, carrying news from one to another, and so conveying it to all parts of the country. But that Mrs. Limber should remain undiscovered by the police, notwithstanding all the efforts they had made, seemed almost incredible.

Whether she had waylaid Fairy herself, or whether she had got a stranger to entice the unsuspecting child while she herself kept out of sight, of course neither Dick nor Luther knew, but they thought the latter the most likely. That Mrs. Limber had got her they had not the least shadow of a doubt; but how to find Mrs. Limber, and through her to get possession of Fairy, were questions for which they could find no answer.

One day, however, nearly a month after Fairy's disappearance, both Dick and Luther thought they had discovered a clue. It came about in this way. Billy Beel— who still purchased all the "weather-glasses" that Dick could manufacture, and who called to give an order for another dozen, "cork ones if possible, but cardboard rather than none"—spoke to Luther and Dick something after this fashion:—

"I dunno ef yer ken mak' owt on it, but it ma' be a true scent for a' that. But Tom Joss tow'd me as 'ow Jim Sykes tow'd him as 'ow Joe Wilks heerd Matt Lane a-tellin' Bob Lark as 'ow he'd seen, on th' Crewe roid, a van the very picter o' Limber's an'a braw lump o' lass spearin' through th' winder, th' image o' Fairy Cob.''

Before this long speech was fairly out of Billy's mouth, Dick had donned his cap, picked up his walking-stick, and was ready for the march.

"Nay, nay," said Luther, "not to-night, lad. Wait till mornin'."

Neither of them, however, slept much that night, and with the first streak of dawn Dick was on the march. The day seemed a long one to Luther, and the second longer than the first, and the third longer than either; but when a week had passed, and no tidings came from Dick, the old man began to feel anxious, and as the days passed on his anxiety deepened and his fears increased. And so a fortnight came and went, and still there was no news of the wanderer, nor sign of his coming.

IX

SUSPENSE

THE WEATHER WAS COLD and winterly, for autumn had vanished early this year, and by the middle of October all the country was covered with a mantle of snow. Luther, standing in the open doorway watching the swirling snow-flakes coming down, heaved a great sigh; and if it was not a prayer that rose to his lips at the same time, it was something very near akin to it.

He was feeling very desolate and lonely. Why he should feel so lonely he hardly knew. Before little Fairy came he had lived by himself for forty years, and he had rarely, if ever, sighed for company, or thought his life particularly hard or cheerless. Why, then, should he feel so lonely now? or why should his home seem so utterly cheerless? He had only gone back to the normal state of things, and taken up the old life again that he had accustomed himself to through so many years.

Yet it was not the same: something had been given and taken, and life could never be again to him what it was before.

"I'm like a man," he said to himself, "as was born blind, and lived i' darkness for fifty year, and then got his sight for ten or 'leven short months, an' then got blind again. His blindness 'ud never be the same again; those months o' seein' 'ud make all the difference, an' make the second blindness all the harder to bear."

Luther's figure of speech was quite to the point. Into his dark and cheerless life Fairy had come like a ray of sunshine. For nearly a year she had cheered him with her presence, warming and supporting those tendrils of sympathy and affection in his nature that were all but dead, lighting up the deepest recesses of his nature, and revealing to him possiblities that he did not know existed before. And now that she had gone life could never be the same again.

Winter never seemed so cold and cheerless till he had seen and felt the beautiful summer. Would it not have been better, then, if summer had never come at all? Would it not have been better for him if he had never seen the fairy child that had gladdened his poor life for one brief year? Better if the fountain of his affections had never been opened, if the chord of his sympathy had never been touched by those little fingers?

No! no! Luther would not admit of that—

> "Better to have loved and lost
> Than never to have loved at all."

That chord of sympathy that little Fairy had struck in his nature was vibrating still, vibrating almost in pain, yet the pain was almost sweet, and he would not have it cease. He would not go back to the old life again if he could. Though anxiety and longing had been awakened with his affection and sympathy, yet the longing and anxiety had their compensation somehow or somewhere— he hardly knew how or in what way.

Before Fairy came he had lived selfishly. Every thought of his had been for himself. And yet his selfishness had brought no gladness into his life, had flung no single ray of blessed sunshine across his path. "In saving his life he had lost it." But the last year had been one of sacrifice—

sacrifice of time and money. He had planned, and laboured, and thought, for another's sake. And yet labour was sweeter than ever it had been before, while the sacrifices he had made were as benedictions, and seemed no sacrifices at all. "Truly it was more blessed to give than to receive."

He thought of all this as he stood in the open doorway, watching the snow coming down—and wondering where Dick and Fairy might be. Thought of the great Master whose words touched his heart so strangely, and expressed his deepest thoughts and feelings as no words of his own could do. And as the evening faded into darkness there rose up into his heart a great longing for some friend greater and stronger than himself, for a heart that was more than human in its sympathy and love, for an arm upon which he could lean in his helplessness and trouble.

Somebody has said that prayer is an instinct, that in moments of great trouble or imminent danger we unconsciously cry out to God for help. Perhaps that is the reason why Luther prayed. Dick had been gone fifteen days now, and no message had come from him since he went, and as Luther watched the eddying snowflakes dancing down, and saw another day rapidly closing in, there rose in his heart a great fear that evil had befallen the lad. In truth, he was more troubled about Dick now than about Fairy. What could have become of the boy during all these weary days and nights? That his quest had not been successful was now a certainty, or he would have retuned long ere this. Perhaps, worn out with hunger and weariness, he had lain down under a hedge somewhere, and was frozen to death.

"Lord help him!" he said aloud; and then he started at his own words: they had passed his lips before he was aware.

"Good job none o' our Freethinkers heard me," he said to himself, "or I'd never heard the last on it;" and with that he closed the door, and shut out the night, and betook himself to his easy chair, his pipe, and reflection. "That prayer must ha' been in my heart afore it shaped itself into words," he said to himself. "I can't make myself up no road."

Luther's pipe did not draw very well that evening, his thoughts were too many and too serious; so he laid it aside at length, and sat staring dumbly into the fire.

How solemn and still the house was! And the loud ticking of the clock echoed through it as though it had been a church. Outside every sound was muffled by the thick carpet of snow, while the wind only moaned occasionally; it never raved or roared. Now and then a low moaning came up from somewhere, then gently died away again in the distance.

"Lord help us all!" No sooner did the words escape his lips that Luther sprang to his feet as though some one had shot him.

"I dunno what's come to me to-night," he said to himself, "I feel as narvous as a baby, an' here I be a-prayin' as though I was a Christian. I almost wish I was. But there, there, what be I a-thinkin' on?" And Luther set to work to mend the fire, which was beginning to burn low.

"I've got a kind of feelin' as though summat was goin' to happen," he soliloquized, "and I shouldn't be a bit surprised to see that boy walk in any minnit,"

Having mended the fire to his satisfaction, he went and opened the door and looked out into the wintry street. Nothing was to be seen, however; the snow was still falling in large thin flakes.

The next moment he had it in his arms.

"This snow ain't a-goin' to last," he said to himself—"never does so early in th' year; but I wish that boy 'ud come." Saying which he closed the door again, and walked leisurely back through the shop into the living-room.

The fire was burning brightly by this time. So Luther seated himself in his easy chair once more, and gazed steadily into the glowing grate. What pictures did he see in the fire that fastened his gaze so intently? Of what was he thinking that he sat so motionless and still? We cannot tell; but he started to his feet at length with an exclamation of surprise.

Was that a knock—a moan—a feeble cry for help? Or was it the wind moaning round the house? Or was it simply his fancy playing him tricks? He held his breath to listen, but no sound broke the stillness save the ticking of the clock.

"I'm gettin' as narvous as a baby," he said to himself again. "But I shan't be a bit surprised if that boy don't turn up yet". And once more he went to the door and opened it.

Nothing was to be seen, however. But, stop! On the doorstep was a bundle of rags half hidden by the snow.

"Hullo!" said Luther, "what's this?" bending low to examine the bundle. The next moment he had it in his arms, and was rushing swiftly into the house. "Thowt he would turn up somehow," he chuckled, as he laid the unconscious lad on the sofa before the fire. "But, dear, dear! I didn't expect him in this state."

It was Dick, sure enough—but, oh! such a bundle of rags and dirt, and so emaciated as scarcely to be recognizable.

Poor lad! He had tramped from village to village, and

from town to town, always buoyed up with the hope of finding his Fairy, yet ever doomed to disappointment. He had walked his shoes completely off his feet, he had torn his clothes into ribbons. By day he had begged a crust here and there to keep him from starving, and at night he slept in outhouses, in hay-ricks, in empty carts or casks— anywhere or in any place that offered shelter, and where, during the hours of darkness, he might hide his heartache and disappointment.

At last he gave up hope. Besides, he was so completely exhausted that he felt he could prosecute the search no further, and so he turned his face towards home. How he ever reached his home he never know. For two days and a night he tramped incessantly—indeed, some part of the distance he literally crawled; but he felt that he dared not stop, that if he once yielded to his weakness and weariness it would be all over with him. He knew when he reached Luther's door, and with one feeble knock he fell senseless to the ground.

When he came to, Luther was bathing his cut and bleeding feet in warm water, great tears running down his wrinkled cheek all the while.

"I'm glad I'm got home, Mr. Luther," said the boy, when he was able to speak.

"And I'm glad too," answered the old man, and that was all that was spoken for some time. Luther did not ask him about his search. He knew that it had been unsuccessful, and he would not by any words of his add to his pain.

Dick lay in Fairy's bed that night, and for many a day and night after, while old Mrs. Podger nursed him as though she had been his mother. At one time it seemed as if the lad was too far exhausted ever to recover again. But he had youth on his side and a strong constitution.

Besides, he had a purpose in life which he felt he must fulfil ere he died. "I'll never die," he said to himself resolutely, "till I've found Fairy."

By Christmas he was quite recovered, and was once more busy at his work. Indeed, he never worked so resolutely as now. But it was not for himself, but for Fairy. Any day he might hear of her, and he would need money to seek her and bring her home. So early and late he was at his labour, and the thought of his lost sister seemed to inspire his genius and give strength and skill to his hands.

During these days he invented a new mechanical toy, which had a great run until some one stole the idea from him and patented it as his own. That transaction, however, taught Dick a lesson. He described it himself "as a reg'lar eye-opener," and the next discovery of his genius he patented himself and so reaped himself the harvest of his brain.

So time wore on. The days gradually lengthened into weeks and the weeks into months, and people began to prepare for Christmas once more. That is to say, November was drawing to its close, when Dick discovered, or fancied he had, a new clue to Fairy's whereabouts. What that clue was, and what the end of it, must be reserved for another chapter.

X

A FRESH CLUE

LUTHER AND DICK WERE both busily engaged in the workshop that was now common to both—Luther on an old pair of shoes, that most people would have regarded as past mending, Dick on a new mechanical toy, from which he was expecting great things. It was nearly noon, and scarcely a word had passed between them since morning. But that was no uncommon circumstance. Luther was naturally a quiet man; and having lived alone so many years, it was the most natural thing in the world that he should remain self-absorbed hour after hour, forgetful of the presence of his companion.

Dick knew well the old man's disposition, and did not care to disturb him; moreover, he was often so busy with his own thoughts as to be in no humour for conversation, even if Luther should feel inclined to talk.

The day in question was cheerless and depressing in the extreme. From a leaden sky the rain had poured unceasingly since daybreak, and there was no sign of it ceasing; on the contrary, it seemed to pour faster and faster as the day advanced, while the wind threatened to blow a gale ere nightfall. Now and then Dick or Luther would look up from his work for a moment, as the raindrops were pelted against the window-panes by a sudden gust of wind, but no remark was made. Each was busy with his own thoughts, and neither cared to start a conversation.

That their thoughts should travel on much the same lines was not to be wondered at. Never a day passed over their heads, scarcely an hour, but they thought of Fairy, and wondered what had become of her.

Every day they hoped—almost against hope—that some tidings might reach them as to her whereabouts; but the days closed as they had opened, except that their hearts grew more and more sick with hope deferred.

During the first few months of her absence they scarcely spoke to each other of anything else; but as time passed on they grew more and more reticent. What had they to say that had not been said fifty—ay, a hundred—times over? It seemed almost childish to be always saying the same things; and so, little by little, the subject was dropped, except on rare occasions. But if they spoke less they thought the more, while day by day the burden of suspense became heavier to be borne.

Several days had now passed since Fairy's name had passed their lips, yet both were thinking of her, both hoping that she was safe, and one at least was praying that the Great Father in heaven would keep the child from harm.

When a neighbouring clock struck the hour of noon, Luther got up from his stool and retired to the living-room to get dinner ready. Half an hour later he called to Dick.

"Come, boy," he said, "dinner's quite ready, so you'd better come an' get it while 't is warm."

"All right," said Dick; "I'm as ready as the dinner is," And a few minutes later he was doing full justice to Luther's plain though substantial fare.

For several minutes the meal proceeded in silence, then, as a fierce gust of wind shook the house, and dashed the big raindrops against the window-pane as it went roaring

73

past, Luther raised his head and remarked,—

"Dreadful weather, ain't it?"

"Horrid!" was Dick's reply.

"Folks as is compelled to be out a day like this is to be pitied," said Luther.

"Ay," said Dick. "I hope little Fairy's snug an' warm somewheres."

"I hope so too," Luther answered, after a pause. "I've not been able to keep the little gal out o' my noodle all the blessed mornin'."

"Nor I," said Dick; "an' I'm fair losin' all patience. I don't think I ken stand it much longer, an' if yer get up some mornin', Mr. Luther, an' find I'm missin', yer may guess I'm off in search o' her."

"But what 'ud be the use o' that?" said Luther. "We'll have to wait till we get some kind o' clue to her whereabouts. To start out on a search wi' nothin' to guide yer 'ud be a fool's arrant, 'cause while yer were goin' north she might be goin' south."

"Ay, I've thought o' that too," said Dick. "An' yet it seems to me the longer we wait the less chance we have of findin' her; we may stay 'ere till we're dead an' buried, an' never find out nothin' 'bout the little gal. An' I tell 'ee what, Mr. Luther I can't stand it."

"But ye'll have to stand it, if ye can't find her," said Luther. "I'm as anxious 'bout her as ye are, but till we get some clue we'll 'ave to bide, an' bide in patience."

"I'm wearied o' waitin' for clues," said Dick; "an' if I don't 'ear summat soon, I'm off."

"What, wi' nothin' to guide ye?"

"Ay! We've waited a whole year for a clue, an' none's come, so what's the use? I'm goin' to search for a clue some o' these days, an' if I've to tramp the world over

74

I'll find her."

"The world's a bigger place than ye thinks," said Luther, with a shake of his head.

"Can't help that," answered Dick. "She's my sister, you know—my own sister, On'y think o' it. Here be I, snug, an' warm, an' comfortable, an' my own little Fairy a-sufferin' nobody knows what. I tell 'ee, Mr . Luther, it fair drives me mad sometimes. I lies awake at nights a-listenin' to the wind a-roarin' an' moanin' round the 'ouse, till for all the world it sounds like little Fairy out in the darkness crying for somebody to come an' take her in; an' I tell 'ee, Mr. Luther, I can't stand it much longer."

"I wouldn't put a straw in yer way," said Luther; "an' I'd be willin' to spend the last copper I has in the world in tryin' to find her. But yer knows, Dick, last year ye nearly killed yerself, an' did no good. An' what chance is there of you doin' better if ye tried again?"

"I dunno," said Dick; "on'y I've been axin' the Lord pretty 'ard lately to put me in the way o' findin' her, an' I've got a kind o' feelin', somehow, as if I started out He'd put me in the right track."

To this Luther made no reply. If he had no faith in Providence himself, he had not the heart to shake the faith of the boy. Moreover, his own feelings had undergone a wonderful change of late, and just at present he did not know what he believed. That he was no longer an avowed sceptic was quite certain. He had given up attending any of the meetings of the "Freethinkers," for their creed no longer satisfied his intellect or his heart. He had also found much in the New Testament that just suited his need, and responded to the deepest yearnings of his nature. In short, Luther had become in matters of belief a little child, and

75

was anxious to be led into the path that was right and true. So he made no reply to Dick, yet the lad's words set him thinking again. And so silence fell between them; and Dick picked up a page of an old newspaper that was lying on the floor, and began to spell out a paragraph, the heading of which attracted his attention. This was rather a slow process, and by the time he had thoroughly mastered its meaning Luther was fast asleep.

The paragraph that had attracted Dick's attention was headed with the words, "Serious Circus Accident," and went on to state that during an entertainment given by a travelling circus in Birmingham, one of the tight-rope dancers, that went by the name of "The Flying Fairy," missed her footing, and fell from a great height. She was picked up insensible, and conveyed at once to the hospital, where her injuries, which were understood to be serious, were at once attended to.

"Flying Fairy," mused Dick to himself. "I wonder now if it's our Fairy? Oh, dear! I do hope it ain't our Fairy as is hurt. An' yet" (scratching his head), "and yet, if it are her, I may be able to find her—that's if she's livin'. Oh, dear! I'm sadly boggled. I'll ax Luther what he thinks on it.

But a snore from the old man testified that he was fast asleep. Not wishing to disturb him, Dick read through the paragraph again, then turned to the date of the paper, and discovered that the accident happened at least two months before.

This fact decided him what to do. "There ain't no time to be lost," he said to himself. "If she ain't dead she'll be well by this, an' ready to leave if they ain't already took her away. I'll go at once—this very day!"

And up he started, and in a very few minutes had

changed his clothes, thrust into his pocket all his little hoard of money, and was ready to be off. Still Luther slept on; and Dick was at first undecided whether or not he should acquaint him with his intentions.

"I've half a mind to let him sleep," he said to himself; "for if I don't, as likely as not he'll try to stop me from goin'." But a little more reflection convinced him that such a course would be unfair to the old man, who was Fairy's true friend as well as his own.

"Mr. Luther," said he, touching the old man lightly on the shoulder; "I'm off."

"Off! off!" said the old man, starting up. "Who's off? what's off?"

"I ain't got no time to explain now," said Dick. "But here's the paper. You can read all about it. I'm off to Birmingham to find out."

"Not to-day, surely," said Luther, rubbing his eyes. "Why, it's near two o'clock. You'd better wait till to-morrow mornin'."

"No! I've made up my mind to go right away," said Dick. "An' don't expect me back again till yer sees me. I've got money 'nough to last me a week or two, wi' care. So don't worrit 'bout me. If I don't find Fairy in Birmingham, I'll start somewhere else. I'm bound to find her somewheres."

"Well, good luck to 'ee, my lad," said Luther. "An' I hope I'll be seein' yer back soon, an' little Fairy along with yer."

"I'll be back by Christmas, any road, if I'm livin'," said Dick. And the next moment he was gone.

The rain was still coming down as persistently as ever, while the wind was blowing half a gale, as Dick pushed his way through the almost deserted streets towards London

Road Station.

"Any train to Birmingham?" said Dick, rushing up to the first porter he caught sight of.

"Ay, ay. You're just in time for the two-ten express," was the answer. "Have you got your ticket?"

"What ticket?" said Dick.

"Why, your railway ticket, to be sure," laughed the porter.

"Have I to get a ticket?" said Dick, in some bewilderment. "Yer see, I've never been in a train yet."

"I s'pose you've got money enough?" said the porter.

"Oh, aye, I guess so," said Dick. "How much will it be?"

"Six an' 'levenpence ha'penny," was the answer. "But you get in and give me the money, and I'll run and get your ticket, for there's no time to lose."

A few minutes later, amid the banging of doors and the shrieking of the engine, the train glided slowly out of the station. On past houses, houses on every side, with their roofs shining in the pelting rain. Still on, but swifter now, till glimpses of country, bare and sodden, stretched away hither and thither, and swollen rivers wound in and out, and patches of wood on desolate hill-sides looked black and forbidding in the dismal rain.

Yet Dick enjoyed it all immensely. It was a new sensation to him to be whirled through the country at the rate of forty miles an hour. It gave to him a sense of exhilaration, and made him forgetful of the anxiety that had been pressing upon his heart so long.

Poor boy! He did not know where night would find him, nor how his search would end. It was well for him that he did not. Had he known, he would not have whistled so gleefully as the train went hurrying past.

Meanwhile Luther was working away very industriously at his mending. Yet somehow he was restless and ill at ease. He was conscious all the while that he was alone, and somehow loneliness was not so congenial to his feelings now as it used to be. He felt as if he wanted some one to talk to. He had worked away all the morning in silence, exchanging no word with his young companion. He had no wish to talk—had nothing to say. No sooner, however, did he find himself alone than all this was changed. The silence got almost oppressive, and the desire for conversation seemed almost more than he could bear.

"Dear, dear!" he said to himself, "what queer comical critters we be, to be sure. We never val'ee what we've got till we lose it, an' are everlasting a-hankering after things as are out o' reach. When I've got some one to talk to I'm as silent as a church-yard, and d'rectly I'm left alone I'm ready to burst up for want o' somebody to have a crack wi'. I'm fair moithered to know what's come to me lately. If I'd been threescore years younger I should believe I'd got changed at nuss—I should for sure."

The old man smiled at the idea for a brief moment, and the next moment he was stitching away more vigorously than ever.

"It's that blessed little gal that has done it all," he said to himself, stopping suddenly short. "She set me on another track somehow—stirred up this old heart in sich a way that I'll never be the same man again. Ay, an' I never want to be, that's more. Oh, dear! I'd give all I've got to have the little Fairy back again. The Lord prosper the boy."

Here Luther started from his stool as though something had stung him.

"I wish I could find out the right o' this," he said to

XI

AN ACCIDENT

DARKNESS HAD BLOTTED OUT all the landscape long before Dick reached Birmingham, but the rain had ceased, and though the wind was blowing a gale, he did not mind that in the least—on the whole, he rather liked it. He was young and strong, and there was something exhilarating in fighting the fierce wind that made the telegraph-wires above his head "ling" again, and almost drown the roar of traffic.

Every one he inquired of knew the hospital he was in search of, so he hurried on without waste of time, except an occasional pause to inquire if he was on the right track. As he neared the building in which so many sick and suffering lay, his excitement became intense. It seemed to him as if all the trouble and anxiety and suspense of the past year were crowding themselves into a single moment, and the weight of them seemed almost more than he could bear. His heart thumped against his side as though it would leap out of its socket. His breath came in quick, short gasps, while his legs trembled so that he had to lean against a lamp-post for support.

Before him rose the great stone building, with its many windows, and a low light burning in each, and as he paused for awhile, that his legs might cease their trembling, a dozen questions rushed through his mind, which he found impossible to put aside.

"Was it likely that the little circus dancer that had got hurt was his Fairy? And if so, what then? Perhaps she was dead!—dead and buried; or perhaps she had recovered, and Mrs. Limber had taken her away! Or if she were still in the hospital, would he be allowed to see her and take her away? Was it not too late in the day for visitors to be admitted? and if so, where should he spend the night?"

These questions, and a dozen others, crowded into his mind as he stood with one arm around the lamp-post, watching the twinkling lights in the tall building and trembling in every limb. He longed to know the best or the worst, as the case might be; and yet somehow, now that he had reached the end of his journey, he felt that he had not courage to go and ask the question on which hung all the hopes of his life.

"I didn't think I wur sich a softy," he said to himself at length, trying to steady himself in the fierce wind that roared up the street. "I'm wus nor a baby." And with that he tried to put a bold face on the matter, and made a rush across the street.

Was it the wind that caught him, or did the trembling in his legs come on again, or did he get bewildered by the the shouts that fell on his ear, "*Keb! Keb!*" Certain it is that he made a sudden stop in the middle of the street, then made a spring to escape a cab that was full upon him, without noticing another cab that was being driven at full speed in the opposite direction. Then followed a moment of confusion, a sudden blow, a flash of light, a Babel of voices, a trampling of hoofs, a swift rush of darkness, and then—oblivion!

Both cabs pulled up suddenly. The fares jumped into the street with the question, "Hullo, what's up?" A crowd of people gathered quickly; and last upon the scene came a policeman, who elbowed his way through the crowd, and shouted in stentorian tones, "Now, out of the way, can't yer! what yer crowdin' on?"

At the bidding of P.C. 87 the crowd gave way and poor Dick, mud-bespattered and wholly unconscious, was dragged from underneath the cab.

To hurry with him across the street to the adjoining hospital was the work of a few minutes only, and then the policeman returned to his beat, and the crowd dispersed as quickly as it had gathered. The traffic of the street rolled on as swiftly as before, and Dick was forgotten. Was there a Providence in this? Who shall say?

"Is it a serious case?" asked one of the nurses, after the doctor had examined the unconscious lad.

"It is impossible to say just yet," was the answer. "So far I can find no other injury than the broken arm, though this long coma would seem to indicate something more serious."

All that night Dick lay quite unconscious, with closed eyes and pallid lips. He might be dead, he lay so still and looked so white. But as the morning dawned a change came over him, but whether a change for the better or the worse it was difficult to say.

The first sign of a change was a rapid twitching of the eyelids. Then he opened his eyes quite wide, and stared around him, but there was no look of intelligence in his eyes, and when at length he began to speak, his words were thick and incoherent.

Later in the forenoon, however, he began to put sentences together; but the nurse declared she could make no sense of what he said. He talked about weather-glasses, and shoes, and gluepots, and Luther; but what Martin Luther had to do with shoes and gluepots she could not make out.

After a while he became silent again, and closed his eyes as if in sleep, and lay thus for a couple of hours. Then, without opening his eyes, he began to talk again.

"Don't stop me, Mr. Luther," he said; "I'm a-goin' to find her if I has to go the world over. She's my sister, ye knows—my sister Fairy."

At this point a look of interest came into the nurse's face, and she pulled a chair to the bedside and sat down to listen. But Dick started off again to talk about cork, and glue, and pasteboard. He soon, however, came back again to the one engrossing thought of his life—the fate of Fairy.

"I dunno where she is," he went on, "but I mun find her. She's got a mark on her arm like a bunch o' grapes, an' a burn-mark on her foot for all the world like a button."

"What's that, poor boy?" said the nurse, leaning forward and placing her soft hand upon his forehead. But he did not heed her.

"Let her go, please," he said, after some rambling talk about shoe-strings and glue. "Let her go; you's not her mother; you stole her when she wur a little 'un; you're a bad 'un, you are; let her go, she's my sister Fairy. I've tramped all this way to fetch her home."

Then for the next half-hour he rambled on about Mrs. Podger, and Tinker's Row, and model churches, and Luther, in a way that was quite laughable were it not so sad. But true as a needle to the pole, he always came back to Fairy.

"Fairy dead?" he said, opening his eyes wide and staring round him. "Killed in the circus, was she? Oh, Fairy, Fairy, Fairy! wake up an' say ye're better. Oh, no, ye mustn't die! Ye must get better, Fairy, and Mrs.

Limber shall never have ye no more. Mr. Luther'll 'ave a big fire for us 'gainst we come back; an' won't it be jolly!"

So he rambled on hour after hour, till, utterly exhausted, he fell into a profound sleep.

Meanwhile in another wing of the same building was the very object of his search—his own loved Fairy. She was sitting in a low rocking-chair nursing a doll, though in a very quiet and listless fashion.

She has greatly altered since last we saw her. See, she rises as we approach, and now we can look at her and mark the change. How tall she has grown! and how pale she is, and thin! and what a look of suffering there is about her mouth! Such an expression of patient endurance is scarcely natural on the face of one so young. It surely speaks of much suffering in the past—of days and nights of agony.

"Fairy!"

How she starts at the sound of our voice, and stretches out her hands blindly, and turns full upon us her great glorious eyes!

And now it is our turn to start. "What!" we exclaim. "Is it possible? Do you not—"

"No," she answers in low, sad, musical tones, "I do not see you. I am quite blind."

"Oh, Fairy! Fairy! what will Dick say when he knows? But perhaps he will never recover; then he will never know, for surely it will break his heart to find his Fairy *blind*.

Her blindness was quite a puzzle to the doctors. She had sustained some slight injury to the spine in her fall from the rope; but whether the blindness was the result of this, or whether it was produced by the shock to her nervous system, or whether both these causes combined

"My poor child", said the nurse, kindly.

had produced the blindness, it was impossible to say. One thing alone was certain, and that was that she was quite blind, and it almost appeared now as if hopelessly so. At first the doctors thought that the loss of sight was only temporary, but as the days passed on and grew into weeks, and the weeks into months, and there was no glimmer of returning sight, they shook their heads ominously, and expressed their fears that she would never see again.

It was a sad awaking from those hours of oblivion that succeeded her fall.

"Oh, where am I?" she cried, stretching out her hands into the darkness. And the nurse came instantly to her bedside and tried to soothe her.

"You are in the hospital," she said. "You fell from the rope, don't you remember? but you'll soon be better again if you keep quiet."

"But why have you no light?" asked Fairy. "Why do you keep the place so dark?"

"But there is a light, lovely," said the nurse tenderly. "The gas is burning low, but there's quite light enough."

"The gas!" said Fairy. "Where is the gas?"

"Why, there, above your head, my child," said the nurse.

"But there is no gas," persisted Fairy. "I cannot see you. I cannot see my hand," she said, passing it again and again before her eyes.

"Not see your hand?" said the nurse in astonishment.

"No; I see nothing," said Fairy. "All is dark, dark, dark!"

"My poor child!" said the nurse kindly, "your eyes have got hurt. We did not know that. But I'll tell the doctor, and he'll soon make you better. Now don't fret, for that will make your eyes worse. If you can sleep it will be all the better."

"Will the doctor take away the darkness?" asked Fairy eagerly.

"Oh, yes; no doubt he will, if you will have patience," said the nurse soothingly; and with that assurance Fairy closed her eyes, and soon afterwards was calmly sleeping. But when she awoke again to darkness, her grief was pitiful to see.

"I want the day to come," she cried. "It's so very dark, an' its been dark so long. Oh, do drive away the darkness an' let me see."

"We cannot make you better all at once," was the answer. "You're badly hurt, you know; and you must stay in bed for many days—"

"And may I have no light?" eagerly asked Fairy.

"Not yet, my child," was the answer. "Now try to be patient."

Poor little Fairy! She did try to be patient, but it was a hard task. Day by day the doctor and nurse encouraged her with words of hope, and after awhile she seemed to grow reconciled. The darkness did not terrify her as at first. And slowly she learned that the darkness was in herself; that what was dark to her was light to others. In other words, she learned that she was blind.

It was a sad lesson for one so young to learn, but she did not lose heart or hope. Moreover, her very blindness brought her some compensation. She could not go back to the hated life she had left—to the cruelty and misery and fear—until she recovered her sight, and sometimes she felt as if she would rather remain blind than go back again.

Sometimes kind ladies visited her, and read to her out of the Book of books, and talked to her of the love and wisdom of the Saviour. And now and then, when the nurse had a few minutes to spare, she would sit by Fairy's side, and speak to her brave, hopeful words.

"Your loss of sight, Fairy, may be the greatest mercy that could ever come to you," said the nurse one day.

"How do you think that?" Fairy asked.

"Because it may save you from a worse fate," was the reply.

"But yer don't know how hard it is not bein' able to see," Fairy sighed.

"No, that is true," said the nurse. "And yet I am sure it is better to be blind than to be wicked; and who can tell what you might grow to be if you stayed in the circus?"

"If I were only sure I should see again some time," she said one day, after weeks had passed, and still all was dark, "I think I could bear it better."

"But you must not lose heart, Fairy," was the answer. "The doctors are puzzled, but they're not in despair about it."

So day by day helpful, hopeful words fell upon her ears and entered into her heart, and though the outside world was dark to her, within it was growing light. In her affliction she was learning lessons of patience, and resignation, and trust, that she might never have learned had she not been afflicted—lessons that would abide in her heart, whatever might be the future, and that could hardly fail to be helpful in the race and battle of life.

Mrs. Limber came to see Fairy two or three times during the first week of her illness, but finding that the child was not likely to be again a source of profit to her, she determined that if possible she should not be a source of expense, and so one night the Limber caravan moved quietly out of Birmingham, and since then the authorities had not been able to find her.

To speak correctly, the "Limber" caravan was no longer in existence, and had not been for more than a year. Indeed, it was soon after Fairy found a home with Luther Cob that poor old Mr. Limber passed out into the silent land, and soon after Mrs. Limber married Mr. Adolphus Boozer, the principal acrobat of the company. And so while the detectives were making inquiries here and there and everywhere for "John Limber's Circus," Mrs. Limber (now Mrs. Boozer) was laughing in her sleeve, and thinking how nicely she had outwitted them all, while little Fairy was wearing her heart out with grief and anxiety, and wondering why it was Luther and Dick never came to rescue her from the hateful life she was forced to lead.

Now, however, the long bondage had come to an end. Her deliverance had been effected at last, but how differently to what she had hoped and dreamed! Night after night, in the noisy dirty circus, she had scanned the upturned faces, in the hope that Dick or Luther might be among the number, and though they never came, she never wholly lost hope. Each day she said to herself, "Perhaps I shall see them to-night." And it was this one hope that sustained her week after week and month after month. Without it she could not have borne the vulgar gaze of the noisy unwashed crowd; without it she would have pined herself to death.

Now, however, that hope was taken away. If Luther and Dick searched every circus in the land, they would not find her now, while she might never look upon their face again if they came within her reach.

XII

EXPLANATIONS

DURING THE DAY ON which Dick—hurt and unconscious— was admitted into the hospital, Fairy and the nurse had a long conversation together. The nurse began it by asking Fairy if she did not think it strange that her mother should forsake her in such a heartless manner.

"No," Fairy answered quietly; "I ain't at all s'prised at it."

"Not surprised?" questioned the nurse in wondering tones. "Not surprised at your mother leaving you?"

"But she ain't my mother," said Fairy.

"Come, come, Fairy," said the nurse with a smile, "you are joking now."

"No, I's not joking," said Fairy, raising her sightless, pathetic eyes to the nurse. "She's told me lots an' lots of times she ain't my mother. She always stuck to it I was a orphan, an' she used to beat me cruel bad."

"Beat you, my child?"

"Ay, that she did when I didn't please her, an kick me too; and so I runned away."

"And how far did you run, Fairy?" asked the nurse, with a smile.

"Well, not very far the first time," answered Fairy. "A policeman soon picked me up an' took me back again. An' didn't I get it just! I thought she would a-killed me.

"My poor child," said the nurse, kindly, stroking her

soft hair the while.

"But the next time I runned away," went on Fairy, "it was quite dark, an' I runned right agin a lad in turnin' round a corner, a big strong lad he were too, an' so back I goes on the ground; but bless you, he picks me up in a minute, he were that strong. But he were the raggedest lad I ever did see in all my days; but his face! oh, he had a fine face, had Dick!"

"Was that his name?" asked the nurse.

"Ay, Dick Dugdale were his name, an' he lived in Tinker's Row. That's in Manchester, you know. Well, he were kind to me, were Dick. His mother were sick an' very poor. That's the reason he were so ragged, he told me. So you see he couldn't take me home wi' him. So what ye think he did?"

"Well, I have not the remotest idea, Fairy," answered the nurse.

"No, I guess ye ain't," Fairy answered, with a smile, "so I'll jest tell yer. Near by where Dick lived was an old man called Luther Cob; he used to mend shoes an' sichlike, and lived all by himsel'. He had curious ways wi' him, had Mr. Luther; but bless yer—as Dick always said— he were good at bottom. So Dick took me to his house. At first he wouldn't speak to me, an' seemed awful mad, but he comed round after a bit, an' when I told him all 'bout myself, he said I should stay wi' him till he'd found out all' bout me."

"And did he find out?" asked the nurse.

"Ay, that he did," said Fairy eagerly. "He found out that Mrs. Limber stole me when I were a little thing, an' he told her so, and he told her, too, that if she didn't clear out o' Manchester right away, he'd set the pleece on her."

"And did she leave?"

"I guess she did," said Fairy, her face brightening. "I mind how Mr. Luther comed home as pleased as Punch, an' said we shouldn't be troubled wi' Mrs. Limber any more, and wern't I just glad, that's all? Bless yer, I were fair ready to fly; and Dick were as pleased as Mr. Luther; and after that didn't we have grand times!"

"And did you live with Mr. Luther, as you call him, after that?"

"Ay, that I did," said Fairy. "Why, bless you all the folks thought as 'ow I were a relation of Mr. Luther's, an' called me Fairy Cob; and wern't I happy, that's all! Why, we had ever sich a nice house, an' a great big sofa, an' sich roarin' fires when the nights were cold. An' then Dick took to makin' toys an' weather-glasses, an' sichlike; and Mr. Luther 'lowed him to work in his shop. An' I used to help to melt the glue an' put the bits of cork together; an' in the evenings when 't was fine Dick an' I used to go into the park, an' on Sundays we went to church an' chapel, an' to the ragged-school besides. Oh, dear, those were grand times!"

"But how did you come to leave?" asked the nurse.

"I didn't leave at all," said Fairy, "I were jist stole. Mrs. Limber got a man to steal me; an' afore I knowed a'most, I were back again in the old circus."

"But if your friends were so kind, I wonder they did not fetch you back again," said the nurse.

"I 'spect they did search as much as they could 'ford," said Fairy, sadly. "But, ye see, the circus had a new name, poor old Mr. Limber were dead, an' Mr. Boozer were the master; an' so you see they wouldn't think of searchin' for Boozer's circus."

"Ah, yes; that will explain it, very likely," said the

nurse; "so we'd better inform Mr. Luther that you're here."

"Oh, if yer would!"said Fairy, clasping her hands, and turning upon the nurse her sightless eyes. "Oh, if yer would I should be so happy!"

"Then we will do so most certainly," said the nurse. "If you had only told me before, he might have been written to long since."

Fairy did not reply to this. She might have said that she never before had an opportunity, but she did not say so. Moreover her blindness had made her reticent. She could not see the faces of those around her, and often she did not know whether only one person or many persons were near; and so, not knowing who might be listening, she was often silent when she longed to speak.

"What did you say Mr. Luther Cobb's address was?" said the nurse, coming towards Fairy with pencil and paper.

"Manchester," said Fairy eagerly.

"Yes, but what is the number and name of the street?" said the nurse. "Manchester is a very big place, you know."

Instantly Fairy's eyes fell.

"Oh, I don't know that," she said. "I never thought of askin'. I know Dick Dugdale lived at Fourteen Tinkers' Row, an' Mr. Luther's wer'nt far away."

"But in what part of the city is Tinkers' Row?" asked the nurse.

"I don't know that it were in any part pertickler," said Fairy; "it were jist in Manchester."

"It's a very vague address," said the nurse; "I'm afraid it will find neither of them."

"Oh! I reckon it will," said Fairy eagerly. "I could

94

find it as easy as anything, if I were there an' had my eyes."

"Very likely," said the nurse, with a smile. "But there, I'm wanted. Anyhow, Fairy, we will do our best to find your friends, so don't be down-hearted." And with that she was gone.

It was the nurse who had been waiting on Dick that wanted her.

"I say, Janet," she commenced, "is not that little blind girl to whom you have been talking called Fairy?"

"Yes," was the answer. "Why do you ask?"

"Another question first. Has she got a mark on her arm like a bunch of grapes?"

"Yes, she has."

"An' a burn-mark on one of her feet?"

"Yes; a round scar the size of a shilling," was the reply.

"Then it must be her," said the first speaker.

"But what do you mean, Frances?" the other asked.

"Why, that poor boy that was run over last night has been rambling on nearly ever since about his sister Fairy. How some Mrs. Limber stole her, and how she has a mark on her arm, and another on her foot, such as you have described. All this has been mixed up with wild talk about cork and glue and Martin Luther, that I have not been able to make much sense of it. But it seems very clear that the lad has come to Birmingham in search of his sister."

"Well, this is strange!" said the other, and she proceeded to narrate her conversation with Fairy, and the conclusion they both came to in the end was that the lad was none other than Fairy's friend Dick Dugdale.

This matter was set at rest early next morning. After a long and refreshing sleep, Dick awoke fully conscious, and stared around him with wondering eyes.

"Bother my buttons," he soliloquized, "what's the

meanin' o' this, an' where in the name o' Judas Hiscariot 'ave I got to" and with that he attempted to scratch his head, but a sharp twinge of pain made him pause and grind his teeth. "Hello," he soliloquized, "this are a pretty kettle o' fish, an' no mistake: timber on my arm, an' calico round my yed. If this aren't a caution, my name's not Dick Dugdale." A little reflection, however, made matters more clear.

"Hi! that's it, you may depend," he said to himself. "I got spilled by that keb, that's sartin clear. I mind tryin' to clear it, but missed it, I s'pose. It didn't miss me, any'ow. And then?—Well, now, I can't make it up no road after that. All my senses got knocked out o' me, I 'spect. Well, there wern't much on 'em to start wi', so that were a small job. An' so I got brought here. That's it, as sure as Moses. This is the hospital, I'll be bound. I wonder, now, if Fairy's here?"

Just then the nurse came up to his bedside.

"If you please, marm, is this the hospital?" he asked, without giving her time to speak.

"Yes, my lad," she answered; "are you better?"

"Ay, I reckon I'm pretty middlin'," he replied. "'Ave I been a bit out o' shape?"

"You were run over by a cab the night before last," she answered.

"Ay, I guessed as much," was the reply. "I've been tryin' to reckon it up this hour or so, an' I'd about come to that way o' thinkin'."

"I'm glad you are so much better," she answered. "And now, would you mind telling me your name?"

"Oh, ay," he answered quickly. "My name's Dick Dugdale, an' I come from Manchester. I seen in a newspaper how a little girl called Fairy'd got hurt in a circus, an' was took to the hospital; an I thought, maybe, it were my sister Fairy who'd got stole, an' so I comed off right away. Were this the hospital she were took to?"

"There was a little girl who had got hurt in a circus brought here some time ago," the nurse answered.

"An' is she here still?" Dick questioned eagerly.

"Yes, my lad, she is here yet; but I do not see how she can be your sister, for this little girl has no brother."

"Oh, but Fairy didn't know as how I *were* her brother when she got stole," Dick answered, "an' I didn't find it out till after she were gone."

And Dick proceeded to tell all the story with which the reader is already acquainted.

"Well, certainly that puts another face on the matter," said the nurse when Dick had finished. "Anyhow, when you get a little better you shall be taken to see this little girl, and then you will know whether she is your sister or not."

"But can't I go an' see her to-day?" Dick asked rather fretfully. "I'm sure if she's Fairy she'll be mighty glad to see me, an' I'm a'most starved for wantin' to see her."

"My poor boy," said the nurse kindly, "I'm afraid you will not be able to get out of bed for many a day yet, so you must try to be patient. No one will run away with the little girl, I can assure you."

"Oh, dear!" sighed Dick; "them's very hard lines after waitin' so long."

"Well," said the nurse, "we must hear what the doctor says first, and as soon as he gives permission you shall see her."

So with this assurance Dick had to be content. It was near noon when the doctor visited him, and poor Dick thought the forenoon the longest he had ever spent. It was a dark, depressing day, without a single gleam of sunshine, and scarcely, indeed, any daylight. Hour after hour he lay there with closed eyes, rolling his head from side to side, and thinking only of Fairy. His own fate never seemed to trouble him, expect in so far as it had to do with his sister. He manifested no surprise on the discovery that his arm was broken, and very little concern about it. If he had found Fairy, that would satisfy his heart, and he would not mind a few bruises and broken bones.

Dick submitted to the doctor's examination without a moan, though it taxed to the very utmost his power of endurance. Once or twice he could have shrieked with pain, but he set his teeth firmly together, and was silent. If he had to suffer, he had made up his mind he would suffer like a man. He had never been a coward yet, and he was not going to begin now.

"You are a brave lad!" said the doctor when he had completed his examination, "a very brave lad; and now I think we have found out the extent of the injury."

"And can I get out of bed to-day?" Dick asked eagerly.

"Well, hardly, I think," the doctor said, with a smile; "but what do you think about it yourself?"

"Well, I'm mighty sore," said Dick; "but I wouldn't mind a bit o' sufferin' if I could only see Fairy."

"Ah, well!" said the doctor, who had been let into the secret, "as you cannot go to see the little girl, why, she must come to you. There can be no harm in that, so I will mention the matter to the nurse directly."

"And shall I see her to-day?" Dick asked, the tears welling up in his eyes.

"Yes, my lad, you shall see her this afternoon. Why not?"

"Oh! then," said Dick impulsively, "you're the best

doctor I ever heerd tell on, an' I'm mighty 'bliged to yer!"

"Now, don't get exiting yourself about the matter," said the doctor, "or I may countermand the order." And with that he was gone.

"He's a brick, anyhow!" said Dick to himself, when the doctor had left him. "An' now I wonder how long it will be before Fairy is here?"

From bed to bed he watched the doctor pass, up one side of the long ward and down the other, and when at length he passed out of the door Dick heaved a great sigh of relief.

"He'll tell the nurse now," he said to himself, "an' Fairy'll soon be here."

It was easy enough for the doctor to tell him not to get excited, but to carry out the advice was a very different matter. For more than a year his heart had been hungering for news of his sister and for a sight of her face, and now the intense longing and suspense had reached its climax. In a few minutes now and they would be brought face to face. And yet there was one agonizing doubt—she might not be his sister, *his* Fairy, after all.

And so he lay with his eyes fixed upon the door, and listening for the welcome footfall that should tell of his Fairy's approach.

XIII

AT LAST

I HAVE SOMETHING TO tell you Fairy, which I think will interest you very much."

The child was sitting in her low rocking-chair, fingering her doll in a listless fashion, and rolling about her beautiful sightless eyes, as though searching in the dark void around her for a single ray of light. Upon her pale thin face was a wistful pleading expression that had become habitual of late, as though the hard lesson she was learning was not mastered yet, nor, indeed, ever could be.

She brightened up instantly, however, at the nurse's words, and greeted the speaker with a smile though she made no reply.

"You remember hearing of the lad that was run over in the street the night before last?" went on the nurse.

"Oh, yes, poor lad!" said Fairy. "Is he better?"

"Yes, he's very much better; the broken arm is the only serious matter, and that will soon be right again."

"I'm very glad," Fairy answered. "Have they found out who he is yet?"

"Well, Fairy that's just what I've come to talk to you about. He says he comes from Manchester, and that he's on the search for a little sister of his who was stolen away from her home more than a year ago."

Fairy was upon her feet by this time, her eyes dilated, her lips trembling, her breath coming in quick short gasps.

"Is it Dick?" she cried out at length. "Is it Dick Dugdale? Do tell me this very minute."

"Come, come, Fairy, don't excite yourself, my love," said the nurse. "It *is* Dick, and what do you think—"

"Oh! let me go to him this very minute," she cried, without heeding the nurse's question.

"Yes, my dear, you shall go to him, only I wanted to tell you that he has discovered that you are his sister: you were stolen away when you were little more than a baby. Now, what do you think of that?"

"Oh, that *is* delightful!" she cried, her face beaming with pleasure. "Then Dick is my brother! Oh, isn't it jolly to have a grand brother like him? Now let's go to him at once." And taking hold of nurse's hand, she marched away with quick, eager steps.

By some strange oversight no one had told Dick of Fairy's blindness, and so he had to learn the sad truth from her own lips. It was well, perhaps, that it was so. With every sense keenly awake as he lay with his eyes fixed upon the door, he heard the double footfalls along the corridor, saw the door slowly open, and then held his breath. The nurse entered first, and then came Fairy holding her hand.

"Could it be Fairy?" was the thought that flashed through his mind. "So tall, and pale, and thin!" With eyes almost starting out of their sockets, he raised himself in the bed, forgetful of bruises and broken arm, searched her face eagerly for another brief moment, and then burst out, to the astonishment of every other inmate in the ward.

"Glory! an' it's Fairy after all!"

Fairy started at these words, as though struck with sudden pain. The next moment she had let go the nurse's hand, and was rushing swiftly and blindly towards the bed. Fortunately nothing stood in the way, and in another moment her arms were around her brother's neck and she was crying softly, her face pressed close to his.

"Oh, Fairy! Fairy!" he cried, and for several minutes no other word was spoken. Dick did not try to check her tears, while he felt that if he attempted to say anything more the words would choke him. Fairy was the first to break the silence.

"You are so good to come," she said. "I'd a'most given up hopin'."

"An' it's by a mighty queer fluke I did get here at all," he said, trying to speak cheerfully.

"Oh, ay," said Fairy; "I'd a'most forgot you'd been hurt. I'm so sorry, Dick."

"Oh, I don't mind that a bit," he replied, "now I've found you. But you have altered, Fairy; I hardly knowed for a moment if 't were you, yer so tall an' thin."

"Be I?" she said sadly. "An' you, Dick, be you altered?"

"Well, what do you think?" he said. "You can tell best."

"Oh, Dick! Dick!" she cried, "do ye not know? Don't you see? Ain't they a-told you?"

"Told me what?" he said, lifting up her face with his hand and looking at her.

"Oh, Dick! I cannot see you," she said: "I'm blind, quite blind!"

For a few moments he seemed as though he were struck dumb, then he wailed out, "Oh, no, Fairy, don't say that! oh, no, don't! I couldn't bear it."

"We must bear it, Dick," she said simply, "It's been all dark ever since I comed here."

"An' can't yer see *me*, Fairy?" he moaned, as if unable to realize the truth of her words.

"No, Dick, I cannot see yer," she said, "but I know ye're here."

"Then I don't want to get better," he said, dropping his head back upon the pillow; "I'd rather die. We'd better die, both on us, Fairy; better die an' be buried in the ground."

"I said that first 'long," she answered, "but not now. I don't mind anything now for you'll take care of me, won't yer, Dick?"

"Take care o' yer, Fairy!" he said slowly, and his whole countenance underwent a change as he spoke. *"Take care o' yer!"* The thought seemed like a new revelation to him. He had something indeed to live for now.

"Look here," he said, starting up on his elbow. "I didn't mean that what I said just now. I take back them words 'bout wanting to die. I ain't a coward, Fairy, an' I take 'em back. Do'e hear, Fairy? I take 'em back. I don't want to die, an' I ain't a-goin' to die either, if I knows it. Take care o' ye, Fairy! that's jist what I'm a-goin' to do. Won't I work when my arm gets right again, that's all! An' we'll go into the park in the evenin's as we used to do, and my eyes shall serve for both on us. An' I'll tell ye about the flowers an' them things in words so good that ye'll think ye sees them yourself, Fairy."

"I know yer will, Dick," she said simply. "An' Mrs. Boozer'll never steal me no more, now I'm blind."

"Mrs. Boozer! who's she?" he asked.

"Mrs. Limber as was," she answered; and then Fairy went on to tell some of her experiences, while Dick closed his eyes to listen.

A little later Fairy's hand sought his face, and slowly and carefully the soft fingers traced each lineament of those features she knew and loved so well. This pathetic action enabled Dick to realise more fully than he had yet done the sad truth that his Fairy was quite blind. And it was only by a strong effort of will that he kept himself from sobbing outright; yet for her sake he repressed his tears, lest her soft fingers should find them on his cheek, and she be troubled in consequence. But when at length the nurse returned and took Fairy away, he let his grief have vent, for it would no longer be stayed. Hour after hour, with his face buried in the pillow, he sobbed as though his heart would break. It seemed such a cruel fate, that now he had found his Fairy she could not see him. What a strange meeting theirs had been—he helpless and she blind! and was this the answer to all his prayers and tears?

But he grew more reconciled at last, and tried to think that all might be for the best, though he could not see how. If Fairy did not murmur, surely *he* ought not to do so. If *she* was patient, *he* had no right to give way to despair. On the contrary, it was his business now to cheer her all he could, and not to depress her with his own grief. So when she came again next day to sit with him for a while, she found him full of hope and cheerfulness. He only made one direct allusion to her blindness, and then it was to say that she might get better in time and recover her sight. Not that he had much faith in his own words. "For there was no Christ now," he thought, sadly, "to walk in human form among the sick and blind of earth, and with a word or touch to make them whole." And somehow he had got the impression that blind people never recovered their sight, except by a miracle or something very little short of it.

Fairy made no reply to Dick's hopeful words, for she did not expect now that they would ever come true. Moreover, she did not want to-day to talk about herself. She wanted to hear about Luther, and all that had happened since she left. And he was quite ready to answer all her questions and tell her all she cared to know.

Sitting there by his bedside, with her little hand in his, and the well-known tones of his voice in her ears, all the past came vividly before her. She saw the little workshop, and the living-room behind, with its big sofa and cheerful fire. She saw Luther in his easy chair, with his pipe between his fingers, and Dick at work in the lamplight with his bits of cork and pot of glue. She almost saw herself standing on a chair to set the tea-things, while Luther smiled, well pleased, to see how handy she had grown.

Several times the tears came into her eyes as she thought that only in fancy might she see those things again, or in dreams of the night. But with a hasty hand she brushed away the wilful tears and tried her best to be cheerful, and on the whole succeeded well.

Poor Dick had to lie in bed much longer than was at first anticipated, and though now and then he grew terribly impatient, no one ever heard him complain, and when Fairy was with him he was as cheerful as any one could wish.

So the days passed on, and if Dick's recovery was slow it was also sure; while Fairy seemed like another child after her brother's advent. The look of melancholy passed away from her face as if by magic, the colour came back to her pale cheeks once more, and her whole demeanour was marked by cheerfulness and content.

At Dick's request no communication had been sent to Luther. "He'll not worrit," he said, "He thinks I'm big enough to take care o' myself, an' he knows I've got a bit o' money, an' I told him afore I left that if I didn't find

Fairy, I shouldn't come back till Christmas Eve, so it'll be all right."

"My! but won't he be glad to see us?" said Fairy, clapping her hands and smiling brightly.

"That's just it," said Dick. "We'll give the owd chap a right good surprise, an' won't he grin? My stars an' stockin's! I think I see him now a-scratchin' his pate an' laughin' all over his face."

"It will be jolly," said Fairy, her face all aglow with anticipation.

"Ay, Fairy; there's on'y one thing as'll make him sorry."

"But he'll soon get used to that," said Fairy cheerfully. "When he sees as I don't mind so very much, he'll not mind either, I reckon."

"He'll not be able to help mindin' a little," said Dick. "We can't none o' us help mindin' at bottom, though yer know, Fairy, it may be all for the best. So there ain't a mite o' use in worritin', is there?"

"Not a bit," she answered. "An' I'll be able to find my way 'bout the house, as well a'most as if I could see; for you knows, Dick, I know where everything's kept."

"Oh, ay," he said, "you'll manage famously, and we'll all be as happy as ducks in a thunder-storm, see if we ain't."

Fairy was quite ready to assent to this view of the case, and there the talk ended for the time.

As the day drew near when the doctor thought it would be safe for them to take their departure, their excitement and enthusiasm became contagious. Not the smallest objection was raised by the authorities to Dick's taking charge of the little blind girl. The evidence that Fairy was his sister was so straightforward and conclusive that no one even thought of raising a doubt on the question, and so at length it was fixed that on the Twentieth of December Dick and Fairy should leave.

During the three months that Fairy had been in the hospital she had won the sympathy and affection of most if not all the ladies who visited that institution from time to time, and when at length her somewhat romantic story was whispered abroad, the interest manifested in her visibly deepened. Dick was also raised to the rank of a small hero, and received a share of public attention that was almost distressing to him.

But the attention in some instances was accompanied by very tangible gifts, the last received being two first-class railway tickets from Birmingham to Manchester.

These kindnesses were very grateful to both Dick and Fairy, and in their simple way they thanked their bene-factors as well as they knew how.

At length the Twentieth dawned cold and grey, but as the morning advanced the weather brightened a little, and by noon there were actually a few gleams of sunshine. But neither Dick nor Fairy troubled about the weather—their hearts were too full of other things for either rain or cold to influence them.

A little before noon they were helped in to a cab at the door of the hospital, and were driven quickly away to the station; but they neither of them felt that they were fairly on their way to Manchester till they heard the whistle shriek and felt the train gliding smoothly out of the station.

"Hoorah!" shouted Dick in his excitement. "We're fair off now, Fairy. Won't Luther cut a caper when he sees us?"

But Fairy's only reply was a squeeze of his hand; her heart just then was too full for speech.

"But my stars!" said Dick, who could not keep quiet anyhow, "we're like gentry, riding in a first-class carriage. Ain't we swells, just?"

So he chattered nearly all the way, with an occasional snatch of a comic song, while Fairy nestled close to his side with one of her hands clasped in his, and waited anxiously for the end of the journey.

XIV

WELCOME HOME

MEANWHILE LUTHER, LOOKING ANXIOUS and troubled, was seated in his little shop, engaged in his usual occupation. Of late he had not given himself much time for rest and reflection. He had found that work was the best antidote against the anxiety that was beginning to pray upon his mind.

When Dick said that "Mr. Luther would not worrit about him" he made a mistake. He evidently had not sounded the depth of the old man's nature yet; for Luther did not carry his heart upon his sleeve, and much as Dick had discovered of his kindness and sympathy, he had not discovered all.

Every day of the lad's absence had been to Luther one long anxiety. Dick was his first thought when he got up in the morning, his last ere he dropped off to sleep; and sometimes he felt positively annoyed that he who had lived all his life for himself and by himself, having no one to care for him and no one to care for, should now in his old age be worried half to death by these two orphan children, who had not the remotest claim upon him, and for whom he was not expected to feel the smallest concern.

But whether expected or no, he *was* concerned. That was just the rub: the problem he could not solve. If they had been his own children he could not feel more anxiety respecting their whereabouts, or more earnestly long for their return.

Sometimes he thought he must be getting into second childhood. This was first suggested to him by one of the fraternity of "Freethinkers," and had stuck to him like a burr ever since. Luther had been so long absent from the meetings and debates of the "Freethinkers," that one of their members came to see him, to ascertain the reason of his long absence.

"Fact is," said Luther, "I'm growin' sceptical."

"Growing sceptical?" said the other in surprise. "What does the man mean?"

"Why, I mean that we're a narrow, bigoted sect," said Luther.

The other gave a scornful laugh at this.

"You can laugh as much as you like," went on Luther, "but it's fact for all that—we think our creed contains all the truth in the univarse."

"Why, man," said the other, "we ain't got a creed; we're above creeds."

"Bah!" said Luther, "don't talk rubbish. We've got a creed as much as any Baptist or Methody or Churchman, an' the first article in the creed is this: 'I believe that there is no God.' "

"Well, you accept that, don't you?" said the other.

"No, I don't," said Luther stoutly.

"Then you are no longer a Freethinker," was the somewhat angry reply.

"Humph!" said Luther: "that's just where you make a mistake. I be free now, an' I'm not going to tie myself down to your creed any longer. I'm going to search for myself; and that which agrees wi' my reason an' finds an echo in my own heart, that, God helpin' me, I'm going to hold to."

"God helping you, eh?" said the other, with a sneer.

"Why, man, you are getting into second childhood, so it's useless further debating the question with you. Good night."

"Good night," said Luther; and once more he found himself alone, but with the sting of the man's sneer rankling in his heart.

It was not very pleasant to think that perhaps he was growing childish, that his mind was failing with his body; and yet if it were so, he could hardly wish it otherwise, since the last two years of his life had been the best and holiest—ay, holiest—since he had left his *first* childhood so far away in the past.

Some such thoughts as these were passing through Luther's mind on the afternoon in question, when he was startled by the rattle of a cab along the street. This was such a rare occurrence that Luther lifted up his head in astonishment, and peered eagerly out of the window, to ascertain, if possible, what it might mean. Hand-carts were common enough, and occasionally a rickety machine drawn by a donkey might be seen; but so rarely did Luther or his neighbours indulge in the luxury of a cab, that the appearance of a four-wheeler in the neighbourhood was quite an event.

On came the cab, however, at a rattling pace, and then pulled up suddenly in front of Luther's shop.

"Gracious!" exclaimed the old man, springing to his feet. "What on earth is up?"

Before he had time to open the door, however, he heard Dick's voice shouting, "Here we are, Mr. Luther! Look alive! Didn't I say I would find her if I had to search the world over?"

"Mercy on us!" said Luther, tugging hard at the door, and forgetting in his excitement to lift up the latch, "if it ain't Dick!"

Fortunately the cabman was not so excited, and lifted the latch from the outside, and Luther was in time to see Dick help Fairy out of the cab. For a moment or two he stood stock-still, bewildered and speechless. He recognized Fairy in a moment, notwithstanding the change that had come over her; recognized also the other fact that she was blind. The manner in which she groped with her hands and rolled about her beautiful but sightless eyes was only too conclusive evidence of the sad calamity that had befallen her. In another moment he had rushed forward and caught her in his arms.

"Oh, my little Fairy!" he said huskily, "an' have you come home like this?"

"Never mind, Uncle Luther," she said cheerily, "you'll soon get used to it."

He made no reply to this; he only kissed her gently, not daring to trust himself to speak.

"Oh, this old sofa is jolly!" she said as soon as Luther had laid her down. " 'T is fine to get back again, and shan't we be happy all together!"

"Will yer be happy?" he said, kissing her again.

"Oh, ay, ever so happy!" she answered. "Won't you, uncle?"

"I don't know," he said huskily. "It's very hard."

"It ain't nothin' so hard as it was," she said; "an' I expect it's all for the best."

"Do you think so, Fairy?" he asked simply.

"Ay," she answered. "They all of 'em said that very likely the good God sent the blindness to save me from something worse."

"I don't understand it," he said humbly.

"No more do I," she said; "but I guess it's all right."

"What makes my little Fairy think so?" he asked tenderly.

"I don't think so," she said; "I feel so. I didn't feel so first 'long, but I do now."

"It's beyond me," he said, more to himself than to her, "beyond me altogether." And then Dick appeared upon the scene, having had a long dispute with the cabman about the fare.

"Now, Mr. Luther, didn't I tell yer I could find her?" said Dick in his boisterous fashion.

"Ay," said the old man quietly. "I'm very thankful to have yer both back." But there was a touch of inexpressible sadness in his voice—Fairy's blindness had evidently touched him to the quick.

"Yer don't talk very cheerful, anyhow," said Dick.

"P'r'aps not," he answered in a low tone; "Fairy not being able to see troubles me above a bit."

"Ay," said Dick, in a lower tone, "it's a bad job, but we'll have to make the best on it."

"If you get fretting you'll make me sorry," said Fairy, "so I hope you'll not talk that way." And with that she slipped off the sofa and began groping round the house. "I want to find where everything is kept," she said, "an' then I'll soon be as handy as I used to be."

Luther watched her with eyes that were very dim, notwithstanding he continually brushed his hard hands across them, but the mist would gather in spite of himself. Had she been sad he would have done his best to cheer her, but her very cheerfulness smote his heart as nothing had ever done before.

It was soon whispered abroad in the neighbourhood that Dick had returned, bringing Fairy with him, and that the latter was quite blind. Poor old Mrs. Podger, who rarely ventured out now, was one of the last to hear of it; but when the news was conveyed to her, she rushed downstairs at a rate that was no less astonishing than it was perilous, and rushing into Luther's house, she caught Fairy in her arms and had almost smothered her with kisses before Fairy could well understand what it all meant.

"Ye'll allow Mrs. Podger to put yer to bed to-night, won't yer?" said the old woman at length.

"Oh, ay, if you wish," said Fairy brightly.

"Ye'll need a little help first 'long," said the old woman, "an' I'll be very thankful if ye'll let me be eyes for ye now an' then."

"I'll be very thankful too," said Fairy, and so it was settled.

After Fairy had gone to bed that night Mrs. Podger came downstairs with a face beaming with pleasure.

"It's her, safe enough," she said.

"Of course it's her," said Luther.

"I mean it's Florrie," said Mrs. Podger, "Florrie Dugdale—bless 'er little heart! I'd rather seen what I have this blessed day than I'd have a hundred pound!"

"An' yer look it," said Dick.

"Do I?" said the old woman brightly. "Well, I 'spect I does. That blessed little gal have been like a big stone on my heart these seven years, an' I've fretted no end over my carelessness. But, thank the good Lord, it's her, safe enough."

"In course it's her," laughed Dick. "Nobody ever said 't wern't her."

"But I wanted to see the marks wi' my own een," said the old woman, "an' I've seen 'em, an' I tell 'e what, I'm fain ready to fly."

"Oh, lor'!" laughed Dick. "On'y think on it, Mr. Luther—Mrs. Podger a-flyin'! Wouldn't she cut a purty figure? I should imagin'—we'd like to see yer make a start, Mrs. Podger."

"Don't make fun on an ould woman," she said, trying to look hurt.

But Dick only laughed the more. Not so Luther, however; his heart was too heavy, his regret too keen, for mirth. In all his long and cheerless life nothing had ever so affected him as the blindness of this little child.

He never slept a wink that night. He could only think of Fairy and wonder at the strange Providence that had sent her such a sad affliction. Like the refrain of a familiar song, Fairy's words haunted him through all these silent, sleepless hours—*"Likely the good God sent the blindness to save me from something worse."* But was it likely? that was the question he debated with himself. "Did God send the blindness? and if so, might He not also restore her to sight? Ah, if He only would!" And Luther thought of the man that was born blind, and of Christ, the marvellous healer, who restored to him his sight. "Oh, if He would but come again and heal this little child!" was the thought that rose in his mind. But, alas! He had gone away from earth long ages ago, and there was no Christ to dwell among men today.

No Christ today? How did he know that? Did not this very Christ say that though He went away in bodily form, He would come again in spirit to abide with His people for ever? And if that were so, was not this very Christ still dwelling on earth? Was He not present to heal and save?

"Oh, dear! if I were only certain about it!" sighed Luther. But, alas! he was not certain. He was still in the borderland of doubt and uncertainty. Before him he saw the promises arching the dark horizon of his life like a rainbow of light and beauty, something as yet afar off, and that could not be touched by a human hand.

Yet that glorious bow was nearer to him now than when first he saw its light. Unconsciously the old antagonism of his nature had broken down, and he was being led by a hand he did not see into that kingdom which is righteousness and peace.

XV

LIGHT IN DARKNESS

IF LUTHER DID NOT get reconciled to Fairy's blindness, he soon grew familiar with the fact, and after a few days, her pathetic groping in the dark ceased to pain him as at first. In a few days, also, she got so handy, and so easily found her way about the house, and was withal so cheerful and content, that Luther felt he had no right to be melancholy—on the contrary, that he ought to do all he possibly could to cheer the child, who was evidently doing all she could to cheer him and her brother Dick.

If Christmas was not characterized by any very boisterous mirth, it was on the whole a very pleasant time—very different to the sad Christmas of twelve months before. In the morning both Dick and Fairy went to church, and in the evening the latter repeated to Luther all that she could remember of the sermon, to which the old man listened with evident interest and pleasure.

By the new year Dick had quite recovered, and set about his work with an earnestness and zest that he had never before known. He had plenty of orders on hand, to which he gave his undivided attention from dawn to dark. But the evening of each day was given up to making experiments in new toys, or in improving previous inventions. In this work he laboured quite alone, for neither

Fairy nor Luther could render him any assistance. Luther could mend a shoe as neatly as anybody, but when it came to a matter of invention he was nowhere. So while Dick was taxing to the utmost his inventive faculty, Luther would be frequently sitting in his easy chair, with Fairy on his knee, reading to her out of the New Testament—the only book in the house that would bear reading twice over.

Fairy's favourite portion was St. John's Gospel, and the old man, always ready to humour her wish, read to her as often as she asked him, and the portions she liked the best. He had no thoughts of himself in this—never stopped to ask himself what influence the reading of that book might have upon his own life. It was enough for him that it was Fairy's wish, and to deny her anything that she might desire was not to be thought of. And so evening after evening he read to her those wonderful words that for centuries have been sweeping over dead spirits like a breath of life. He rarely made any comments of his own. Now and then Fairy would ask him for his opinion, and set him thinking; but in the answers he gave he was always careful not to weaken the child's faith by speaking of his own doubts.

So time passed on. Winter gave place to spring, and spring blossomed into glorious summer, and now Dick redeemed his promise made to Fairy in the hospital. Evening after evening, when the weather was fine, he took her into the park or into the quiet country lanes, away from the strife of the noisy city. Leaning on her brother's arm, she walked firmly and fearlessly by his side, and many of the people they met from time to time had no suspicion she was blind.

On those occasions Dick did nearly all the talking. He

never forgot that while beautiful things were all around him, all was dark to her, and so he told her of everything they passed, and gathered wild flowers for her, that she might enjoy their fragrance if she could not see their beauty.

To Fairy these were blissful times. She loved to hear her brother talk, for on the whole he could talk well, and by the aid of her imagination she could easily realize all that was passing around her. Sometimes, too, he spoke to her of his hopes and dreams for the future. He was already in comfortable circumstances and had saved a a little money, while one of his pet toys was nearly completed, and he was anticipating for it a great run when it got fairly known. And while he spoke, Fairy—with both hands within his arm—would turn up her sweet patient face to his, as if she could see the play of his features and the sparkle of his eye.

No girl was ever prouder of her brother than she was of Dick, and, hugging his strong arm, her face would glow with pleasure, while he unfolded to her his beautiful dream of hope.

"You know, Fairy," he said, speaking of his new mechanical toy, "I'm goin' to take out a patent for it when it's finished."

"What's a patent, Dick?" she asked.

"Well, I ken hardly make it clear," he said. "But it's gettin' the right of it made fast to one's self, if you ken make that out."

"No," she said, "I can't make it out very well."

"Well, it's this way," he said. "If I get a patent, nobody'll be able to copy it, or have the right to make one like it; or, if they do, they'll have to pay me something for every one they make."

"Oh, I see now," she answered.

"Yer see, Fairy, the last good one I made I got nothin' by it, for one of those big makers copied it, and then took out a patent for't as his own. An' now I can't make my own toy without payin' him. But I ain't goin' to be sold a second time, I can tell yer."

"I wouldn't if I was you," she said, encouragingly. "An' won't they be sold when they find you've got all the right?"

"I guess they will," he said, his face glowing with enthusiasm.

Poor Dick was very much disappointed, though, when in September he sought to take out the patent for his now completed toy. He had no idea that it would cost so much money, or that there was such a ridiculous law in existence, the only object of which seemed to be to cripple genius and put a stop to invention.

But Dick was not to be dicouraged. He calculated that with care and economy he would be able to save sufficient money in another year, and he could afford to wait that time, or for two years if needs be. So he schooled himself to patience, and as he had no new invention to occupy his attention he gave the evenings of the following winter to work of another kind.

He was already able to read very well, but in writing and arithmetic he was sadly deficient. So he set himself with all diligence to learn.

Luther, who had always been something of a student, and was far better informed on most questions than people would have given him credit for, undertook to be Dick's teacher, and was very soon surprised at the ease and rapidity with which Dick mastered the subjects that were set before him. He committed the multiplication table to memory in an incredibly short space of time, and was into the compound rules, as Luther said, before one had time to look round.

And so the days passed on, and winter gave place to summer, and summer to winter again, and winter once more was being chased away by breezy spring, before Dick's hope was realized. During all those long months he had worked as he had never worked before, never losing sight of the one purpose of his life, never bating one jot of heart or hope, cheered all the while by his blind sister, who was always patient and ever ready with a word of sympathy and encouragement.

"It's neck or nothin'," said Dick, on his return, after securing the patent. "I've spent every penny I've got in the world."

"It'll be a case if it misses fire," said Luther.

"Ay, it'll be a bad job," said Dick; "but I'm prepared for the worst, and if I lose all, why, I'll start again. I told dear old mammy, when she was livin', that wi' 'perseverance, cork, an' glue,' I'd make my fortune, an' I'm goin' to do it yet."

"Ay, that you will," said Fairy impulsively; "an' it's time enough to talk about losin' all when you are certain all's lost."

This sage remark was hailed with a loud "Hear hear" from Dick, while Luther smoothed her shiny hair with his hard rough hand, and declared she was quite a philosopher.

Dick did not lose all his money, however. He was soon able to make liberal terms with a large toymaker for the manufacture of his favourite and before the year was out found himself in possession of an income that exceeded his fondest dreams.

"Misfortunes never come singly" is an old saying, which, however, is quite as true of successes. Before that summer was over there came a joy into their hearts and home that no money could purchase. And that joy arose from the fact that Fairy could once more see. For a long time she had been able to distinguish light from darkness, and for several months past the light had been growing brighter, but she had kept the knowledge to herself, afraid to buoy up the others with hopes that might never be realized.

Now, however, the dark cloud that had obscured everything so long, and which for months past had been growing thinner and thinner, had at last actually broken, and she was able to distinguish objects passing before her—not clearly—oh, no! Still there was the dim outline, the blurred shape figured upon her vision.

She was in Luther's shop when she made the discovery. It was a bright fine day, and she had turned her face toward the window, as she loved to do when the sun was shining. For a long time she kept her eyes steadily fixed on one spot. At length she said, speaking very quietly, .

"Is there anything hangin' before the window, uncle?"

"Hanging before the window?" he said, looking up in surprise. "No, Fairy, there's nothing hanging there. Why d' ye ask?"

"Well," she said, speaking very slowly, "it's like a bright cloud there," pointing to the window—"all but one square place nearly in the middle."

In a moment Luther had sprung to his feet, as though something had stung him.

"It's right, Fairy!" he exclaimed excitedly. "One o' the panes is gone, an' I've stopped the square with leather."

"Oh, then, Uncle Luther, I can see," she said, her face beaming.

"My darlin'!" he cried, and he caught her up in his arms, "are ye certain?"

"I think I be," she said quietly, "unless I'm dreamin'."

"Bless the Lord, then, ye're not dreamin'!" he said, setting her on her feet again. "But try some other place." And he held up his hand before her. "There, Fairy, d'ye see anything now?"

"Ay," she answered, "something as covers nearly all the window, like a big hand."

"That's it! that's it!" he cried excitedly. "Ye're getting round, for certain. But let's go to Dr. Benson, he's clever about eyes."

And so to the doctor's they went, leaving house and shop to take care of themselves; for Dick was away, and was not expected back till evening.

"It's not a case for medicine this, or the surgeon's knife," said the doctor. "The injury that produced the blindness is beyond the reach of either. But evidently Dame Nature is repairing the injury, and so her sight is returning. 'Remove the cause and the effect will disappear'."

"And you think her sight'll come back all right?" said Luther eagerly.

"I should think it is likely," said the doctor.

"That'll do," said Luther. "I'd rather that than a thousand pounds." And he and Fairy started off home again.

Two strange things happened that evening. The first was, Fairy was heard to sing again. During the years of her blindness she had been quite cheerful and seemingly content. Now and then she laughed, and laughed right heartily, but no note of song ever escaped her lips. This evening, however, the fountain of her joy burst forth into singing. Luther listened in astonishment, while in clear sweet notes parts of an old hymn she had learnt at the ragged school were warbled forth, filling all the room with melody:—

> Away, my needless fears,
>   And doubts no longer mine:
> A ray of heavenly light appears—
>   A messenger divine.
>
> "Thrice-comfortable hope,
>   That calms my stormy breast:
> My Father's hand prepares the cup,
>   And what He wills is best."

It was well Fairy could not see Luther's trembling lip while she sang, or she might have stopped; but, all unconscious of the old man's emotion, she sang on, pouring out her gladness and gratitude in notes of praise. When the singing ceased, however, he stole quietly upstairs, and dropped on his knees by the bedside and began to pray. That was the second strange thing that happened. "Oh, Lord!" he said, "I can't help it. My heart's near bustin' up for very thankfulness. Thou hast done it all. I see Thy goodness, an' I praise Thee for it. I thank Thee for her blindness now. It's been a blessing to us all, but chiefly to me. Her coming to me was good, her goin' away was good, her blindness was good, an' now that she can see again, that is best of all. I believe now that Thou didst send her to lead a poor blind old sinner like me to Thyself. And now, Lord, I thank Thee—not that there's any merit in my thanks, for I can't help it. But if Thou wilt help me for the future, I'll do my best to serve Thee."

Dick returned just as Luther came downstairs, with his eyes still moist, and his wrinkled face radiant with pleasure and gratitude.

"Hi, Mr. Luther! what's up?" said Dick. "Ye look as 'appy as a duck up a pear-tree."

"That's cause I be happy, boy," said Luther.

"Ah!" said Dick, stopping short in the middle of the room. "Owt happened?"

"Ay," said Luther, triumphantly. "Fairy can see again."

In a moment Dick's hat had struck the ceiling, while he himself gave a spring that astonished Luther.

"Hold, boy!" he cried, "or ye'll be goin' through."

"Never mind that," said Dick; "but where's Fairy?"

"Here I be," exclaimed Fairy, coming out of the little pantry.

"An' can ye see?" he cried, throwing his arms around her neck and kissing her again and again.

"Just a little, Dick," she said, and then she began to tell how for weeks the darkness had been getting thinner and thinner.

"Well, that's right down good of Him," said Dick, when Fairy had finished.

"Good of who?" asked Luther.

"Why, the Lord, to be sure," said Dick. "I've axed Him every day since I knowed Fairy was blind to let her see again some time, an' He's done it, you see."

"Ay," said Luther solemnly. "I didn't believe in Him once, nor in Providence, nor in heaven, nor any of them things, but I believe now. I've been like Fairy. I've been blind, an' blind more years than she. But the Lord has opened the eyes of both on us now, an' we ought to be very thankful."

"Well, I guess we be," said Dick.

Ay, I hope so," said Luther. "An' now for our supper, which Fairy's got ready, an' by then—why, I guess it'll be time for bed."

XVI

CHANGES

FAIRY RECOVERED HER SIGHT more rapidly than any one ever anticipated; and by Christmas she could see almost as well as ever she could in her life. Three happier people in all Manchester, ay, in all England, could not be found than were Luther, Dick, and Fairy that Christmas; and as Dick was now comparatively well off—indeed, he considered himself rich—there was no lack of good cheer.

Since Fairy had recovered her sight Luther had always said grace at table, but this Christmas Day they *sang* it. Fairy started the tune in her clear rich treble, Dick piped a bit of tenor, while Luther brought up the rear in a cracked and quavering bass, and then they set to work not only with good appetites, but also with thankful hearts, to enjoy the good things that had been provided.

Dick declared at the close that it was the best dinner he had ever had in his life.

"That's because I cooked it," said Fairy.

"I reckon it's because we're all happy an' thankful," said Luther; "for there's nothing like thankfulness for making things taste nice."

"Oh, well," said Dick, "I wish, any road, I'd a bit more room for that puddin', but I ain't, so I'd as well give over fust as last."

Had any one looked into that humble home that

Christmas evening, he would have seen a pretty picture. On the big roomy sofa sat Dick and Fairy, the latter holding her brother's hand, her eyes sparkling, her face aglow with pleasure; while in his easy chair was Luther, with a light on his wrinkled old face that scarcely seemed of earth. He had been telling them how happy he was in his old age, and how good God had been to him in leading him out of the darkness in which he had so long dwelt, into the clear light of faith and love.

"Never you bother yourself with them Free-thinkers," he said to Dick. "There's no comfort in it, my lad, nor hope. It's all, 'Nay, nay,' from first to last. It's all a-pullin' down, an' buildin' nothin' up. If ye ask for bread, they give 'e a stone, an' if ye ask for a fish they give 'e a serpent. They call themselves 'Freethinkers,' but that's all nothin'. I'm a freer thinker now than ever I was. I'm free now to accept the truth as satisfies the hunger of my soul. 'T ain't a question of proving always: there's lots of things one can't prove, an' yet he knows somehow that they're quite true. They fit his nature an' his need, an' satisfies him altogether. Stick to that, lad, which satisfies yer heart's yearnin' an' meets yer hope of a future life. Stick to that which teaches ye to be honest, an' pure, an' true. Ay, stick to that, an' ye'll not ail much."

Much more to the same effect he said, but we have not space for any more of his reflections. Suffice it that they made a deep impression on Dick's mind, and helped in no small degree in leading him into the fold of Christ.

Before retiring that night they had what Luther called a "tryo." Fairy commenced by singing a hymn or carol she had heard that morning in a neighbouring chapel:—

> "Hark! the glad sound, the Saviour comes,
>   The Saviour promised long.
> Let every heart prepare Him room,
>   And every voice a song."

Luther listened with closed eyes while she sang, and happy grateful tears, that would not be stayed, welled up into his eyes and rolled down his cheeks. When she had finished, Dick took up the New Testament, and read the second chapter of St. Matthew's Gospel, and then Luther wound up the "tryo" by offering prayer. So ended that first Christmas Day after Fairy had recovered her sight.

Three days after, Dick made an announcement, "The cottage next door," he said, "comes empty this week, so I have taken it for workshops—that is, the downstairs rooms. We shall want the upstairs rooms for bed-rooms. Fairy must go to school with the new year. I'm going to make a lady of her. You needn't laugh, Fairy, I mean it," he said, turning to her. "We ain't going to live in this place always, either; an' you'll have to learn to play the piano, an' knit fancy things, an' all that. We'll have a woman to do the work of the house. I've nearly settled it all, an' it's too late now to object."

Nobody, however, thought of objecting, and so it was settled.

What need is there that we should linger over this period of their lives? Fairy was as eager to learn as ever her brother was, and so she threw all the energy of her nature into her lessons, and, as might be expected, made rapid progress. True—for her age—she was at the bottom of the school, but no one taunted her with that, for all her schoolmates knew how she had once been blind.

So four years passed away—happy, peaceful, prosperous years. Fairy, growing in mind and beauty, was blooming into womanhood. As for Dick, he considered he had been a man for many years past, and certainly the "down" upon his upper lip testified that he was no longer a boy. "Happy years," we said. And in truth they were. During the winter evenings Dick and Fairy pursued their studies together, by their own fireside; but when summer came they strolled, as had always been their custom when the weather was fine, into the park or into the country lanes. And people that passed them in their rambles often remarked, "What a nice-looking young couple."

Fairy was always particular about her dress. Her early circus training may have had something to do with it. Be that as it may, she seemed to know by instinct what suited her, and so she always dressed with taste. Dick, however, had no such gift. He never seemed to trouble what he had on, and so Fairy undertook the care of his wardrobe, and made him dress as *she* pleased. The consequence was, Dick's personal appearance underwent a surprising transformation. They had many a laugh and many a joke over the matter.

"You were the raggedest boy when we first met," she said, "that I ever saw in my life."

"Ay, I suppose so," he said, laughing; "but you were always up to the knocker, Fairy."

"And if it hadn't been for me you would go in rags now," she went on.

"Moas likely,—" he drawled with becoming gravity.

"But I've made a gentleman of you," she continued.

"Not the least doubt of it. Under your care I've bloomed into a howling swell."

"No you've not, but you do look respectable."

"My sweet sister, I sit corrected."

"Now don't look that way, Dick, you spoil your face."

"From such a calamity may the good fairies spare me."
And with mock gravity he would seize his hat and march away. And Fairy, with beaming face, would watch him till he was out of sight, proud of the handsome young fellow she called her brother.

At the end of four years Dick planned another change. In the first place, the neighbourhood of Tinker's Row might do very well for workshops, but it was not very desirable as a place of residence. In the second place, he wanted more room to meet the demands of his increasing business; and in the third place, Luther's health had begun to fail, and the old man seemed to pine for the fresh air of the country. So a house a few miles out of Manchester was resolved upon, and at length one was found about a stone's throw from Buckley Station.

It was the beginning of June when they took possession, and the first thing on which Fairy's eye lighted when she got into the house was a new cottage piano. And so great was her delight that the only way she could express it was to sit down and have a good cry. This performance provoked Dick into such unseemly laughter that she got up at length and boxed his ears, and then kissed the place to make it well, after which all went merry as marriage bells. Luther was delighted with everything. The house with its neat new furniture and cheerful carpets; the garden all abloom with flowers; the hedge white with hawthorn; the fields dressed in living green; the valley below sleeping in a golden haze.

"I feel better already," said Luther; "I shall renew my youth like the eagles."

They has been settled in their new home about a fortnight when Dick received a visit that caused him quite a little flutter of excitement. Most of his neighbours had called and seemed disposed to be friendly, so that there was not much likelihood of Fairy or Luther being dull if they cared for company.

On the evening in question, Fairy was seated at the piano playing some dreamy voluntary, while Dick and Luther, under the pretence of reading, were both listening to the music, when the servant announced: "Mr. and Mrs. Robert Baker."

Dick laid down his book and strode toward the door at once, and in another minute had grasped the hand of his visitor in his usual hearty fashion.

"Good evening, Mr. Baker," he said, "I am very pleased—" Then stopped suddenly short, looked at his visitor curiously for a moment, hesitated, then burst out: "Excuse me if I'm mistaken, but you are not 'Chips,' are you?"

"Ay," said Chips, laughing all over his broad, homely face; "all that's left of him, at any rate."

"Well, there's a good deal left, anyhow," said Dick. "But come in; I am delighted to see you. And this is your wife?"

"Ay," said Chips, blushing, "we should have called sooner, only, to tell you the truth, we only returned yesterday from our wedding tour."

"Well, I *am* delighted to see you," repeated Dick. "This is my sister Fairy. You never knew her, I reckon; but Mr. Luther, here, you must have known very well."

"I should think so," said Chips, "most of us lads knew him."

Then followed a long chat about old times, and early struggles with want and poverty.

"I am a good bit older than you," said Chips, "but I remember you as well as anything."

"And how is Ebenezer now?" asked Dick at length.

"Better than ever he was," said Chips. "Indeed he says he grows younger every year. And as for Joe Wigley, he's my right-hand man. You remember Joe?"

"I don't think I do," answered Dick.

"Well, you must come over and see us, and you'll like Joe, I'm certain. Jenny and I would never have had time to get married but for Joe."

"Don't talk nonsense, Bob," said Jenny, blushing; "but Mr. Dugdale knows you, that's a comfort."

"Ay, but he don't know you," said Chips, with a broad grin. "But do you know, Dick, Jenny and I fell in love with each other at first sight?"

"No; I didn't know," said Dick, with a twinkle in his eye.

"Oh, what a cram, Bob!" said Jenny. "But Miss Dugdale won't believe you I know."

"That I won't," said Fairy, laughing.

Chips' joke, however, had the effect of setting them all at their ease, and the rest of the evening passed away in the most delightful fashion.

Fairy was delighted with our old friend Jenny Pearson, now Mrs. Robert Baker. And Dick was pleased beyond measure to find under such happy auspices an old companion in tribulation. During the bright summer evenings that followed many similar visits were paid and returned. And sometimes of a morning Luther would start off down the lane towards Fern Cottage, to have "a crack" with Ebenezer, or a smoke in the shade of the poplars.

So the bright summer months passed away like a dream. Luther declared he had never been so happy before in his life. He spent nearly all his days out of doors. He loved to watch the cloud shadows on the fields, and the flowers in the garden unfolding their beauties to the sun. Nature, to him, was a constant miracle, and a never-ending revelation of God's wisdom and power and love.

He used to say, sometimes, that if he had always lived in the country, he thought he would never have lost his faith in God. "But in the big towns, nearly every trace of God's finger," he said, "is blotted out."

XVII

AND LAST

SO THE SUNNY DAYS sped on, and no one noted the change that was surely coming. Luther declared that he had taken a new lease of life; yet a close observer, even in those days, would have noted that the old man was not what he once was; there was an undefinable something in his manner and appearance, that too surely betokened the coming end.

But when autumn came, and the chill wind moaned solemnly in the trees, and the brown leaves fluttered silently and sadly to the earth; when the flowers in the garden began to droop their heads, and the evening air was touched with frost, then Luther began to droop and fail.

He would not acknowledge it to himself at first, yet his walks got shorter and his step moved slower with each returning day, till he gave up his ramble altogether, and sat idly in his chair from morning till eve.

So gradual was the change that Fairy scarcely noticed it, and when she did she was not troubled. "He's used to sitting all day long," she said to herself, "an' it's natural he should stay indoors now the weather has got chill."

But Dick, who saw less of the old man, was quick to mark the change, though he said nothing about it to Fairy. He thought it better that she should discover the fact herself.

For many weeks Luther made no allusion to the matter, but when his appetite suddenly failed him, the truth became evident even to him.

One afternoon he said to Fairy, "I should like you to sing to me today, if it's not too much trouble."

"Trouble? oh, no, uncle," said Fairy brightly. "It's no trouble at all, it's a pleasure. What shall I sing to you?"

"Sing the 'Better Land'," he said quietly. "I'm only a child, Fairy; an old man in years, I know, yet only a child."

So Fairy seated herself at the piano, and sang in her rich treble voice the song the old man loved.

When she had done he thanked her in low earnest words, and then repeated to himself the last lines over and over again:—

> "Dreams cannot picture a world so fair;
> Sorrow and death may not enter there;
> Time doth not breathe on its fadeless bloom
> For beyond the cloud and beneath the tomb,
> It is there, my child."

"You are a beautiful singer, Fairy," he said at length.

"Do you think so, uncle?" she said, looking pleased.

"Yes, you are a beautiful singer, and I love to hear you. But nothing lasts here, Fairy."

"No," she said quietly.

"No, nothing lasts," he repeated. "The flowers were very beautiful all through the summer, but they are all gone, Fairy, and the trees are nearly bare."

"Yes," she answered, "winter is coming again."

"Yes," he said, "winter is coming. But there'll be no winter in heaven, Fairy. I've thought a great deal about it lately. The flowers don't die there, and I shall die no more when I get there."

"But why do you talk of dying, uncle?" she asked. "You will not die yet for many a year."

He shook his head sadly, and then answered: "You must not be deceived, my child, for I'm nearly done."

"Oh, no, uncle," she said, getting off the music stool and coming and standing by his chair. "You are not ill, and when spring comes again you will be as bright as ever."

"My Fairy," he said, and he smoothed her shining hair with his wrinkled hand, "when spring comes again *I* shall not be here. The flowers will bloom again, but I shall not see them, and the birds will sing in the trees, but I shall not hear them. I shall be in a better country, Fairy, far away from all pain and sorrow."

Oh, no, uncle! do not talk in that way," she said. "I cannot bear to think of your dying."

"It's best you should know," he said gently, "though it grieves me to give you pain, for I think I've never loved anything in the world as I love you. God sent you to me, my Fairy, to lead me back to Himself."

"I'm sure I have only been a trouble and anxiety to you," she said, wiping away the wilful tears that had started in her eyes.

"Trouble? No, not in the sense you mean. Anxiety? Yes. But that was because you were so dear to me, and I loved you so. But no act or word of yours, my child, has ever given me a moment's pain. No, Fairy, you've been the light an' sunshine of my declining years."

"I'm glad I've been a comfort to you," she said, and she began to cry in earnest now.

"Nay, don't cry," he said, stroking her hair, "don't cry, my Fairy. It will only be for a little while, and then we shall meet again. Once I thought that I should die

137

like a dog: simply go out into everlasting forgetfulness. But to you, my Fairy, under God, I owe the hope that now cheers me on. I see the darkness and the grave, but I do not fear, for beyond I see the light, for God is with me holding my hand."

"Oh, uncle, uncle!" she sobbed, "but I couldn't bear for you to go away."

"He will help you," answered the old man, a bright smile lighting up his wrinkled face. "He will help you, as He is helping me; and if any of my old mates ask after me, tell them it was my last prayer that I might die a Christian. Oh, what should I do now, child, now that the shadows are growing deeper every moment, if I were as I used to be, ere you came to lead me into the light?"

"Oh, I do not know, uncle," she wailed; "I do not know."

"But it's almost easy dying now," he went on; "and though the thought of leaving you gives me pain, yet I know Dick will care for you. He's a noble young fellow, is Dick, and God will watch over you both."

He paused a moment, but Fairy did not speak. Then he went on again.

"I've saved a bit of money, Fairy, and I've willed it you. I know you will use it wisely. It's not very much, but you'll think of it as an expression of an old man's love. And don't put me in a brick grave, Fairy; let the warm, soft earth come close around me—it's a childish fancy, but I think I'll sleep the better, close pressed by the arms of Mother Earth. I don't care for tombstones, Fairy, but if you wish to put up anything of the sort, I'd like it to say that I died in the faith of the Gospel, and underneath let these words be:—

"And a little child shall lead them."

138

Fairy was sobbing now with her arms about his neck, so he ceased speaking, and for a long time only her sobs broke the stillness of the room.

On Dick's return in the evening Luther brightened up wonderfully, and chatted away about the ordinary events of life with all his old interest and zest.

Before retiring, Fairy sang, as she often did Luther's favourite hymn, ending with the verse—

> "Fixed on this ground will I remain,
>   Though my heart fail and flesh decay;
> This anchor shall my soul sustain,
>   When earth's foundations melt away.
> Mercy's full power I then shall prove,
>   Loved with an everlasting love."

Then Dick read a Psalm, and Luther prayed. It was a very simple prayer, in which he thanked God for the mercies of the day, and then commended them all to the mercy and care that are infinite. His "Good night", was more than usually hearty, and his smile as cheery as ever. But when in the morning they knocked at his bedroom door, they got no answer. Getting alarmed at length, Dick opened the door and entered, and found him apparently fast asleep, but, on coming closer, he saw that it was the sleep of death. He must have died without a struggle. He lay on his side with his head upon his arm, his eyes closed, his lips just a little apart. Indeed, he never knew the agony of dying. He closed his eyes and slept, and woke to the light of another morning than ours, and to the joy that is eternal.

Dick and Fairy mourned their old friend's departure with genuine grief, for he had seemed as a father to them; indeed, to Fairy he was the only father she had ever known. But time, the great healer, softened their grief at length, and life's many duties left them no time for needless regret.

And now, what need is there that we should say more? We have no story of love to tell. Such love as there is in our story has been already told. Dick has never seen any one that—in his eyes—is half so fair as Fairy, and he thinks she grows more beautiful every day; while Fairy thinks that there is no man in the world to be compared to her brother, and so is quite happy in his love. What the future may bring, of course, we cannot tell; that we must leave.

Every year Dick brings out some new invention, or adds some novelty to the many that have gone before, and every year his business increases. His home is a perfect little bower of peace and contentment, presided over by the angel of his life—his Fairy.

All Dick's acquaintances know that he is a prosperous man. They all know that he is a genius. They all know that he possesses an amount of dogged perseverance that would succeed anywhere. But none of them knew—not even "Dick's Fairy"—till last year, that he is a poet.

Last year Dick built a new workshop, or manufactory, not far from his own dwelling. He wanted to be nearer home, and moreover, the old shops were wanted by the Improvement Committee, and he was under notice to quit. So he prepared his plans and set to work, and last year the building was completed, and pronounced by competent judges to be a model of its kind. The walls are of brick, but conspicuous over the main entrance is a large stone with an inscription on which his fame as a poet rests. The inscription we give in full:—

Also published by Gallery Press

HER BENNY

Silas K. Hocking

Two homeless waifs, with only their courage and love for one another to keep them going, Benny Bates and his sister Nell face the injustice and hardship of the Liverpool of ninety years ago. While little Nell sells 'fusees' in Paradise Street, 'her Benny' earns a copper by carrying the bags of the gentlemen travellers at the Pier Head. Somehow, with the help of their old friend, Joe Wrag the night watchman, they survive . . . until one terrible day . . .